I0570518

Detroitopia

Book Three:

Unforeseen Consequences

by
Cyrus Vanover

PUBLISHED BY:
Iconic Inkwell

Detroitopia
Part Three: Unforeseen Consequences

Copyright © 2014 Cyrus Vanover

ISBN-13: 978-0692270073
ISBN-10: 0692270078

Printed in the United States of America

First Edition: August 2014

10 9 8 7 6 5 4 3 2 1

Be sure to visit the author's web site for updates on new book releases and other exciting things!

www.cyrusvanoverbooks.com

CHAPTER 1

I AM SUDDENLY AWAKENED from a deep, dreamless sleep. I open my eyes but don't see anything. Everything around me is pitch black. Is it morning, or have I awakened in the middle of the night? I have no idea. I just know that I no longer feel sleepy and that it feels like it's time to get up. Unless my internal clock isn't working properly, I'm guessing it's six or seven in the morning … the usual time I wake up.

I'm in a small room in the Motor City Community Center that Dr. Bradshaw took me to yesterday evening. Returning home was out of the question, he said. It's much too dangerous with the manhunt for me that is currently underway. It isn't the Ritz, that's for sure. When Maggie and I laid our weary bodies down last night, we didn't have any blankets or pillows. Still, it's five star accommodations to me for the safe haven it's afforded us. I'm thankful for it.

I'm not sure if I'm ready for what I'm waking up to. Dr. Bradshaw told me yesterday evening that I will be leading the first attack against the sentries today, but I'm not sure if I'm the right guy for the job. I certainly have my doubts, that's for sure. I close my eyes and try to go back to sleep again, to forget all about what I must face today, but sleep doesn't find me.

Maggie is still sleeping on the floor near me. Even though I can't see her, I can hear the rhythmic sound of her breathing. She went to sleep fast last night. Poor thing has been through a lot lately, and I'm sure she needs all the rest she can get.

I feel around on the floor for the matches Dr. Bradshaw left for me yesterday evening. I find them, take a match out of the pack, and strike it, illuminating the room in a soft, faint glow. It's a simple room with block walls and a concrete floor. The paint that covers the walls is faded, cracked, and peeling. The ceiling is an old, hanging ceiling with mildew-stained tiles from some long-neglected leak. Hanging beneath the tiles is a pair of old fluorescent tubes that no longer have power running to them.

I take the lit match and carefully carry it over to the oil lantern that Dr. Bradshaw left for us. I light the wick and the light in the room grows a little stronger. I can now see Maggie clearly. She's lying on her side on the floor with her mouth open. It's a position that looks terribly uncomfortable to me. I help her roll over so that she's now lying on her back. She closes her mouth, swallows, and her breathing falls back into a steady rhythm. "Get plenty of rest, little one," I say to her. "You've certainly earned it."

I pick up the oil lantern and open the closed door, being careful not to make any noise. The door opens silently. I walk out and close the door quietly behind me. As I look around in the hallway, I see a few rays of light penetrating a boarded-up window. My internal clock is still working. It's morning.

I walk slowly down the hall of the community center with the intent of exploring this large building that I know so little about. Even though I lived near it growing up, it's a place I never bothered to visit prior to Yellowstone when everything was normal. In a city the size of Detroit, it's easy to do. As I walk down the hallway, I imagine the many families and others who visited this place for various reasons. I think of children laughing during the special kids' programs, of politicians speaking to packed crowds about various issues, and all of the many clubs and volunteer organizations that held their activities here. Those days are long gone. This place continues to serve the community, but in a much different way now.

I don't go far until I walk past a door that is slightly ajar. Curious, I open the door, walk in, and hold my lantern up to illuminate the room as best I can. It's a much larger room than the one Maggie and I slept in last night. Other than its size, it looks about the same with its painted block walls, concrete floor, and stained tile ceiling. Something in the far end of the room catches my attention in the flickering light of my oil lantern.

I walk over to the objects and hold my lantern up to them to get a better look. Before me are two Applied Dynamic Technologies Mark III Infantry Suits, the very ones worn by the Detroit sentries. These must be the two suits Dr. Bradshaw and Elise were wearing yesterday. The suits are stretched out on a clothes rack of some kind and the helmets are sitting nearby on a small shelf. I walk up to one of the suits and run my hand across the fabric, as if touching it somehow makes it more real.

"Remarkable technology, isn't it?" I hear from behind me. Startled, I quickly turn around and see Dr. Bradshaw in the doorway holding a lantern. He is light on his feet. As he walks into the room, I notice that his footsteps make no noise.

"I didn't hear you walk in," I say. "You're just as stealthy as if you were wearing one of these suits."

Dr. Bradshaw smiles. "I've developed light feet from years of taking care of so many patients. Did you get plenty of rest last night? You'll be needing all of the energy you can muster for our activities today."

"I did; I feel great. Maggie's still sleeping, though. I decided to let her sleep a little longer."

"You'll need to wake her soon. Elise is preparing a bath for her right now. And one for yourself, too. It looks like it's been quite a while since your little friend has seen a bar of soap."

"She's been through a lot," I say. "I don't think anything in her life has been normal." As young as she is, I seriously doubt that she has any memory of what a normal life even is. Normal for her is about as dysfunctional as you could possibly imagine. Maybe I can somehow help her change that. Maybe.

Dr. Bradshaw walks up to one of the suit helmets, picks it up, and hands it to me. It's incredibly light, as though it doesn't even weigh anything.

"What's it like?" I ask. "Running around in one of these super suits?"

"Oh, remarkable … just remarkable. The capabilities are truly incredible. The helmet doesn't feel stifling at all. The field of view is so wide that you completely forget you're wearing a helmet after just a few minutes. And the information displayed on the heads-up display is incredible, too … GPS location on a map, outside temperature, and so many other things. It'll even tell you how fast your heart is beating, if you really want to know.

"Very interesting," I say.

"You can even have enhanced hearing, if you want. Just look in the direction of the area you want to listen in on and select amplify on the heads-up display menu. The visor tracks the movement of your eyes. To select something on a menu, you just blink twice in rapid succession, like double-clicking a computer mouse. You remember those, don't you?"

"Yes, old school computing," I say.

"Old school," Dr. Bradshaw repeats. "It's the same basic principle."

"Do other sentries in the area know your location when you're wearing the suit?"

"Yes … and no. At least these suits don't have the ability to advertise our positions anymore. I disabled the device that relays location to other suits. The downside to this is that you won't know where the sentries are when they are near you. It had to be done … I didn't have any choice in the matter."

"But what about the invisibility?" I ask. "What's it like?"

"It's about what you'd think. You're there, but everyone walks by you without even so much as looking your way. You'll get to see for yourself soon enough. Elise is going to give you a rundown of the suit and its capabilities in a little bit. You'll get to put it on and take some time to get acclimated to it before you put it to use this afternoon. But first, let's get your little friend taken care of. If you'll wake her, we'll get her cleaned up."

I suddenly hear a loud, blood-curdling scream emanating from somewhere down the hall. I run out of the room and into the hallway. The screaming continues. It must be Maggie. She probably just woke up and realized she's all alone.

I run down the hall with the oil lantern to the small room where Maggie is, open the door, and rush in.

"I'm here!" I say to her. She looks horrified, as if she's seen something truly awful. I crouch down in front of her, set the oil lantern down on the concrete floor, and embrace her with both arms. I hold her tiny body close to mine. She wraps her tiny arms around me and squeezes me as if she's holding on for dear life.

"What's wrong, Maggie? What's wrong?"

"I woke up and I was all by myself. I thought you left me like Mommy did."

"No way, Maggie. I'm not going to leave you." I squeeze her body even closer to me.

"You promise?"

"Promise."

A few minutes pass and Maggie slowly calms down. Her wailing turns into light crying, then light sniffling, and then nothing. I slowly release my embrace and she does the same. I look into her eyes, and the look of innocence that should be there is nowhere to be found. It has been stolen from her by the hardships she has faced in her short, hard life.

"Maggie?" I say. "What happened to your mommy? Where did she go?"

Maggie sniffles and her expression grows strained, as if she's deep in thought. "I don't know; she just left. She disappeared."

"When?"

"A couple of years ago."

"What happened? Tell me."

"I just went to sleep one night and when I woke up she was gone."

I hug her tight again.

"I won't do that to you, Maggie. Never."

I can only speculate as to what happened to Maggie's mother. Did the man who was intent on killing and eating me do the same to her? It's certainly possible. If he did, at least he spared the child.

I hear a light knock on the door behind me and quickly turn around to see Elise standing in the door. She looks better than I've seen her look since before Yellowstone. She looks positively radiant. She looks like she's just had a bath and she's even wearing clean clothes. Her hair is braided in a single braid going down her back. She is a vision of beauty.

"I'm sorry to bother you," she says in a soft voice, "but I have a bath drawn for this little lady. Is now a good time?"

I look down at Maggie and she appears to be calm now. And there's no denying that she's filthy, too. A good bath is definitely something she could use.

"Yes, it's perfect timing, actually," I say. "Maggie, I want you to go with Elise, okay?"

Maggie nods her head yes.

"She's going to help you take a bath so you'll feel better, okay?"

Maggie steps away from me and then runs over and takes Elise's hand. Elise smiles at me, and then I watch as they both start to leave. Just as they are almost out of the room, Elise pauses and then looks back at me.

"Don't go far," she says. "You're next."

CHAPTER 2

I'VE NEVER BEEN SO NERVOUS about something as simple as taking a bath in all of my life. It's not the bath itself I'm worried about. It's the idea of stripping down in front of Elise and having her see my emaciated, filthy body. I'm interested in attracting her, after all, not scaring her away. I can't help but feel like I'm waiting my turn at the electric chair. I pace back and forth like a tiger in a cage.

I walk into one of the restrooms in this old building and make my way to one of the sinks. They are filthy, and I'm sure they haven't worked in ages. I set my oil lantern on the sink next to me and look at myself in one of the mirrors. The reflection that greets me isn't much to look at. My face is gaunt and unshaven. My hair is long, unkempt, and thinning in places. My eyes have heavy dark circles underneath them. The image I see before me is the result of years of hard living. It's the result of years of fighting for survival.

I step back from the sink and mirror, lean my head down near my armpit and carefully sniff, and quickly recoil at the horrible smell that greets me. *I'm a walking disaster*, I think. *I don't have a chance in the world.* May as well stop worrying about it and just face the music.

I pick up my oil lantern and walk out of the restroom. Just as I start to turn and walk back to the little room Maggie and I slept in last night, I see Elise and Maggie turn a corner and walk in my direction.

I am stunned by what I see. The wild child that went in for a bath earlier has been completely transformed into a totally different person. She now looks like … a pretty young lady. The dirty and torn clothes she was wearing earlier have been replaced by an attractive outfit. I have no idea where it came from. The wild, unkempt hair she had is now clean and it's neatly braided down her back … just like Elise is wearing hers. I was completely unaware of how pretty Maggie is until now. And I also can't help but notice the uncanny resemblance she has to Elise. They could easily be mistaken for mother and daughter.

Maggie runs up to me with a huge smile, holding Carrie Anne, her doll.

"Look Adam!" she says. "Carrie Anne got a bath, too."

I look at the doll Maggie is holding and it does look different. The dirty doll Maggie used to carry around now looks clean, and the eye that used to hang by a thread has been repaired. The rips in her clothes have been mended.

"She sure did!" I say. "I'd say Carrie Anne feels like a new person after getting all cleaned up."

Maggie nods her head. "Uh-huh."

I look up at Elise and she smiles and winks at me.

"Carrie Anne looks just as clean as you are," I say to Maggie. "Look at you!"

Maggie runs her hand across her hair. "Do you like my hair?"

"Love it! You look marvelous!" And she really does. I am still in amazement over the incredible transformation she has just gone through and the new spark in her eye.

"And now it's someone else's turn," Elise says. "Are you ready?"

"As ready as I'm ever going to be."

I turn back to Maggie. "Maggie, can you and Carrie Anne play together for a while in the room we stayed in last night? It's my turn to get cleaned up."

Maggie nods her head yes and then motions for me to come closer to her, as if she has some kind of secret to tell me. I kneel down in front of her and she comes close to me.

"Be sure to use soap and scrub a lot," she says. "You don't smell so good."

I can't help but smile at her. "I will," I say. "I'll be back shortly."

I stand and start to walk down the hallway with Elise to the room she has set up the bath in, wherever that may be. As I walk down the hall, I hear the pitter-patter of little feet behind me. I glance behind me to see what all the commotion is and see Maggie twirling around and around with her hands outstretched, the picture of happiness. Maybe a good bath will do the same for me. I can hope.

I continue walking down the hall with Elise by my side.

"Her doll," I say. "How did you—"

"I asked her last night if I could borrow Carrie Anne to help me go to sleep and she agreed. She told me Carrie Anne would take good care of me."

"I didn't even notice she didn't have it last night. She went to sleep very quickly."

"Well, she doesn't need a doll to protect her when she's got you to watch over her, does she?"

I feel my face flush with embarrassment.

"I took Carrie Anne and washed her and then did a little sewing on her," Elise says. "She'll never look new again, but at least she looks a lot better than she did."

"You seem to be very good at taking care of people."

"Dad says I get it from Mom. She was always doing for others, often while neglecting her own needs."

Elise stops in front of a closed door.

"Here … through this door."

Elise opens the door and walks in. I follow right behind her. It's a small, plain room that is mostly empty with the exception of a small wash tub in the center and a small table near the door with a couple of chairs. Two oil lanterns illuminate what little there is to see here.

"It's nothing fancy," Elise says, "but it will get the job done."

"Oh, I think it's just fine."

I walk over to the tub, look in, and laugh at what I see before me.

"Bubbles?" I ask.

Elise laughs. "Maggie asked for bubbles and I just happened to have some."

I stick my hand in the water to see how warm it is.

"Still warm," I say. "Nice."

"Go ahead … jump in."

I say nothing in reply. Surely she doesn't expect me to strip down and jump in with her watching, does she? I know she's used to seeing a lot of things from all of the time she's spent taking care of sick people, but still …

Elise looks at me with a sly grin. "Don't worry," she says. "I'll turn around."

Elise turns around and I quickly take my clothes off, step in the bubbly water, and sink down into it until the bubbles cover my entire body up to my head. The water feels good … oh, so good. In fact, I can't even remember the last time I had a bath. This has been a long time coming.

Elise takes a chair in one corner of the room, brings it over to the tub and places it right beside of me. She sits down and hands me a bar of soap.

"Start washing," she says.

"With you here with me?"

"Why not? It's not like I can see you with all those bubbles."

"You have a good point. I guess I just didn't expect to have any bath time company."

I reach into the water with the bar of soap and start scrubbing my feet. I can feel the many weeks of built up grime on them start to come off. Elise continues to watch in silence beside me as I scrub. I can't recall ever having anyone watch me bathe before. Awkward doesn't even begin to describe how I feel right now.

"I saw you taking care of those patients," I say in an attempt to break the silence. "How did you learn to use all of the medical equipment?"

"Dad taught me everything," she says. "When Yellowstone erupted, we were nearly overwhelmed with patients. There wasn't any time for formal training. I just jumped in and started helping Dad as best I could. It was a trial by fire. I was up all hours of the day and night taking care of people. I got a few winks of sleep here and there as I could."

"You have some very valuable skills. I'm impressed."

"Don't be. I did what I had to."

I continue to wash as thoroughly as I can, working my way up my body. I'm not sure when I'll have the opportunity to bathe again. Better make this one count. I look down into my bath and for a brief moment, the bubbles part and I can see just how dirty the water is. It's an embarrassing reminder of just how filthy I am.

"What do you think is going to come from all of this?" I ask.

"Well, the goal is to get clean. That's usually how it works."

I laugh, and then Elise bursts out laughing, too.

"What we're getting ready to do today … our plan of fighting back against the sentries."

Elise takes in a deep breath and stares at one of the walls in the room, as if she's contemplating my question. "I don't know," she says. "Hard to say what the outcome will be. I'm more worried about what will happen if we don't fight back."

"That's what I'm worried about, too. Things are getting worse, not better."

I'm now washing my torso and my arms. I look down at the bar of soap I'm holding in my hands. It's covered in a layer of grime ... grime that just came off of my body.

"The way I see it," I say, "we've got absolutely nothing to lose and everything to gain. Who do you think that Darius guy is?"

"Don't know. No one I know has ever seen him. Maybe he doesn't really exist." Elise takes in another deep breath and then slowly lets it out. She looks long and hard at the wall on the opposite end of the room.

"I never did get a chance to thank you for what you did for me," she says.

"What do you mean?"

"How you saved me from what that sentry was about to do to me."

"It's nothing," I say. "Anyone else would've done the same, I think."

"It *is* something," Elise says. "It's a *big* something. It meant the world to me and I want you to know that I'm very grateful for what you did."

I say nothing in response, mainly because I don't know what to say. I wash my scruffy face and then lather my hair with the bar of soap. I dip my head into the water to get the soap out of my hair and then surface again. I look down into the water and see many strands of hair from my head floating around on the surface of the water. I glance over at Elise, and by the look of surprise on her face I can tell that she has seen it, too. I feel embarrassed. I'm falling apart right in front of the girl I've loved for so long and I know she sees it.

Elise shifts around in her chair a bit. "I'll be right back," she says and then quickly gets up and walks out of the room.

I lean back in the tub and enjoy soaking in the bubbly water. I'm finished washing and it feels good to just sit here and relax and meditate. Alone with my thoughts, my mind turns to Mom and Sarah and I become deeply concerned for them … for their safety. I need to find a way to reach them, to let them know I'm okay. If I can get to them, perhaps I can bring them here. At least it's reasonably safe here … I think.

Elise quietly walks back in the room, interrupting my thoughts. She's carrying something in her hand, although I can't tell what it is. She walks over to me, sits back down in the chair she was sitting in just a moment ago, and then leans in close to me.

"Do you trust me?" she asks.

"What do you mean?"

"Do you trust me?" she asks again.

"Of course I do."

"Do you think I would ever do anything to hurt you?"

"No, of course not." And I don't. I've seen her in action, taking care of sick people in her dad's home. I've seen the incredible care she gives each of her patients. I can't help but wonder, though, what this line of questioning is leading to.

Elise holds up a straight razor in her hand, the kind barbers used to shave men's beards with. I'm starting to get an idea of where this is going.

"I trust you," I say to her.

"Lean your head back."

I lean my head back against the edge of the tub. Elise takes the bar of soap and lathers my face. She then brings the straight razor up to my face and then lowers it to my throat. She pauses. I swallow hard. She presses the blade against my skin and then slowly, gently starts shaving my coarse beard. Neither of us utter a word as she makes cut after cut against the thick beard I've been wearing for so long.

"Why didn't you ever stop and talk to me?" Elise asks after several minutes of silence.

"I am talking to you."

"I'm referring to all of those times you used to walk past my house."

Does she know I used to go out of my way to walk past her house just to catch a glimpse of her? If so, how?

"Oh, I was just passing through, usually on my way home," I say.

I hear Elise snicker a little, like she wants to laugh but she's trying hard not to at the same time. She pats me on the arm. "If you say so," she says.

"I was," I say in a tone of voice that says I'm not guilty. Elise leans closer to me as she continues shaving my face. She is smirking. It's a look that says she knows I'm really stretching the truth with her.

"Even though you live about two miles away and my house isn't near any major road?" she asks.

I'm busted. There's no way I can get out of it now.

"How do you know where I live?" I ask. "I didn't think you knew who I was."

"Of course I did. Dad knew your parents when they were younger. He mentions them on occasion, always good things. I think he may have known your mom better than your dad. He talks about her more."

"What does he say?"

"Always good things. I think they may have even dated at one point, although I've never come right out and asked him. Sometimes, when Dad would see you walk by, he would start talking about your mom."

Elise picks up a towel and wipes my face. I reach up and run my hand across my smooth face. It feels good. It's a feeling I haven't felt in quite a while. I'm starting to feel more like a human being again and less like a wild man.

"Nice work," I say. "You have steady hands."

"Steady hands for delicate work. Now, let's do your head."

"My head?"

I could certainly use a haircut, but the idea of shaving my head never even crossed my mind.

"Do you trust me?" Elise asks once again as she looks into my eyes.

"Of course."

Elise takes the bar of soap again and lathers my hair. She then brings the straight razor up to my scalp and starts shaving the long strands off my head. Minutes pass as she carefully removes the unruly mess, leaving nothing behind.

"I used to wait on you sometimes," Elise says.

"Wait on me? When?"

"I would sometimes go outside when I didn't really need to, hoping you would come by. I would make up excuses, like I needed to hang laundry, gather firewood, or something."

I am shocked by this revelation and I'm having a difficult time processing it in my mind. *All that time I wasted by not stopping to talk to her*, I think.

"Why me?" I say to her. It's all I can manage to say.

Elise doesn't reply right away. She just continues shaving my head in silence. Maybe I shouldn't have asked.

"Why not you?" she finally asks after a lengthy pause.

I don't reply, because I don't know the answer. *Why not me?* I think. I don't know. She would've been asking a much simpler question if she had asked me to explain the meaning of life or to reveal the mysteries of the universe to her. Why not me? Good question. I can think of a million different reasons … at least.

Elise makes one last cut against the hair on my head, wipes my head with a towel, and then leans back in her chair as if she's studying me.

"Handsome," she says in a soft voice. Elise reaches into the water and playfully splashes some of it on my face. "C'mon," she says. "You can't sit here all day. We've got work to do."

Elise stands and starts walking toward the door. She pauses just as she's getting ready to walk out, picks up a towel, and tosses it in my direction. I catch it.

"You might need that," she says. "There's a clean set of clothes for you on the table. I borrowed them from Dad. He won't mind."

Elise walks out of the room.

CHAPTER 3

I STEP OUT OF THE TUB AND quickly dry myself off with the towel Elise gave me. I then walk over and check out the clothes Elise left for me on the table. I find a pair of jeans, a pair of socks, boxer underwear, and a simple t-shirt. They are all clean and neatly folded. I put the clothes on and am surprised by how well they fit. And then I remember Dr. Bradshaw mentioning yesterday evening that I should be able to wear the sentry suit he was wearing. We seem to be about the same size.

I leave the room and start walking along the dim hallway to the room I left Maggie in. I'm sure she's fine, but for some reason I want to get back to her as soon as I can to check on her. All of the windows in the hallway are boarded up but cracks in the wood let the occasional ray of light shine through.

I walk past one of the many windows in the building, glance over at it, and see a faint reflection of myself. I stop, walk over to the window and look long and hard at the stranger who is staring back at me. I don't recognize him, although I do have to admit, he looks rather dashing. I run my hand over my shaved face and bare head. I like it. I'll take this look over the wild man look any day.

I continue walking down the dim hallway and eventually find my way back to the little room I left Maggie in. I walk in and find her having a pretend tea party with Carrie Anne. She stops sipping from the imaginary tea cup she's pretending to hold as I walk in and looks up at me.

"Adam! You look different!" she says. "Can I touch your head?"

"Of course."

I lean my head down to her and can feel her running her tiny hands over my bare scalp.

"I like it," she says. "Elise likes it, too."

"Oh, is that so?

She nods her head yes. "Uh-huh."

"How do you know?"

"I just know." Maggie looks at her doll sitting on the floor and then back to me. "Would you care to join us for some tea?" she asks in an obviously fake British accent.

"But of course, my dear," I reply in the most over-the-top British accent I can muster. I sit down on the floor beside the doll and Maggie sits down in front of me. She reaches her hand over to me as if she's handing me an imaginary cup of tea. I reach over to her and act like I'm grabbing the teacup.

"Would you care for a biscuit to go with your tea?" she asks.

"Naturally, my dear."

I pretend to take a sip out of my imaginary cup and then take a bite out of my imaginary biscuit.

"What am I going to do with the two of you?" I hear behind me. I look behind me and see Elise standing in the doorway, with one hand on her hip and a sly grin on her face.

"Oh, we were just—"

"Just getting ready to join me for a practice run in the sentry suits?"

"Yes, of course."

I get up from my position on the floor, start to walk out with Elise, and then pause at the door. I look back to my little tea time buddy.

"I have to go for a while again. You'll be okay here, won't you?"

Maggie nods her head.

"You'll save a little tea and some biscuits for me, won't you, Magpie?"

Maggie's expression turns to one of horror, as if she has just seen something truly awful.

"No, Adam! No!" she says. "I'm Maggie, okay?"

How could I have been so dumb … to call her by the nickname that man used to call her? I've really stepped in it this time. I walk over to her and kneel down in front of her. "I'll never call you that again, okay?"

"Okay," she says softly. She runs over to me and wraps her arms around me in a tight hug. I return her embrace and I can feel her sigh heavily in my arms. I'm glad that she is quick to forgive but I've got to watch myself so that I don't say or do anything to trigger any bad memories.

"Adam?" I hear Elise say behind me. "We really do need to get going. The practice run … it's important."

Maggie and I release our embrace and I stand and turn to walk out of the small room once again.

"I'll save some tea and biscuits for you, ol' chap," Maggie says in her outrageous British accent. She giggles.

"Righto!" I say.

I leave the room.

CHAPTER 4

Elise and I walk side by side down the dimly-lit corridor to the room holding the captured sentry suits. My curiosity over the suits' capabilities is burning and I can't wait to try one on and put it through its paces.

"You've got quite the little friend," Elise says as we walk.

"She has warmed up to me very quickly. I didn't expect that."

"Maybe it's because you treat her a lot better than that man she was living with."

"Her father?"

"I'm not so sure he was her father."

We continue walking at a steady pace, passing room after room, their contents a mystery to me. A few rays of light pierce the dark through cracks in the boarded-up windows.

"She mentioned something about a mom and dad before the man in the shack while I was helping her bathe," Elise says.

"What happened?"

"She wouldn't say. She just clammed up when I tried to talk to her about it. I could tell that it was bothering her, so I changed the subject."

"Do you think that guy killed them and ate them?"

"Can't say for sure but that's what it looks like." Elise points to a room on the right just ahead. "In here."

"After you," I say. Elise walks in the room and I follow right behind her. It's the same room I was in earlier and everything is just as I left it. The two sentry suits are still hung on the display racks, the helmets still on the shelf nearby. They look ready for action even with no one wearing them, as if they could somehow come alive on their own and take on the world.

"They were designed to take on the toughest armies in the world," Elise says, "and we have two of them in our possession. Not bad, wouldn't you say?"

"Not bad at all. The second suit … where did you get it? You only had one suit at the meeting the other day and you said you were going to get more … and now you have two."

"We got the second suit from the sentry you killed when you came to my rescue. We got the second suit thanks to you. Go ahead, try it on."

Elise walks over, takes the bottom half of the larger suit, and hands it to me.

"Go ahead," Elise says. "What are you waiting for? It isn't going to put itself on, you know."

I take the bottom half of the suit Elise is holding and put it on.

"It's much lighter than I expected," I say. "For some reason, I thought it would be heavy."

"So did I, at first," Elise says, handing the top half of the suit to me. "The suit is remarkably light. The engineers had to design it that way so the infantry could wear it for long periods of time without tiring. After just a few minutes, you forget you're even wearing it."

I take the top half of the suit Elise is holding and knock on the torso armor with my knuckles. It's almost hard to believe that something so light could stop a bullet, but apparently it does. I put the top half on, like slipping on a sweater. It's not a perfect fit, but it'll do. With the full suit now on, I walk over to the rack again and pick up the helmet.

"How do I look?" I ask as I turn and face Elise.

Elise gives me a big smile and chuckles a little. "Not bad," she says. "Are you planning on starting a modeling career?"

"I'm planning on fomenting a rebellion. Think I've got a shot at the job?"

"I'd say you've already got the job. Go ahead, put the helmet on. This is where it gets interesting."

I lift the helmet up to my head and put it on. I see nothing but darkness.

"Nothing's happening," I say. "Everything's dark."

"You have to connect the power and data cable."

"Oh, yeah." I reach behind me and find the cable extending from the top half of the suit. I take it and plug it into the helmet. Instantly, the display inside the helmet illuminates the interior in a soft shade of blue. I can't see through the visor; I only see the blue screen in front of my eyes. Just as I'm about to tell Elise I think something's wrong, a message scrolls across the screen:

… Applied Dynamic Technologies …

and then:

… Modern Technologies for a Modern World …

and then:

… Initializing … Initializing … Initializing …

"What's it doing?" I ask. "It just keeps saying initializing over and over again."

"That's normal. It always does that when a new user puts it on for the first time. It takes a moment for it to complete the retina scan. Just give it a moment."

"It's reading my eyes?"

"Yes, it recognizes each user so that it can automatically return to each user's preset settings when he puts it on."

The message on the screen disappears and a new message appears in its place:

... Starting Retina Scan ... Please Look Straight Ahead ...

I look straight ahead and try hard not to move my eyes, but my concentration doesn't last long. I hear a sound coming from somewhere outside the helmet and, instinctively, I move my eyes in the direction of the foreign noise.

"Look straight ahead," a sultry female voice inside the helmet says.

"Whoa," I say. "It talks, too?"

"Sometimes ... when it has important information for you and it determines audio is the best way to deliver it. Did you do something to make it mad?"

"I don't know." And I really don't. All of this is completely new to me and I feel totally lost. I continue staring straight ahead into the blue void of the display, trying hard not to move. Finally, a new message appears:

… Retina Scan Complete … Retina Scan Complete …

"Please state your name," the sultry female voice in the helmet says.

"Adam Reese."

"Please state your place of birth."

"Detroit, Michigan."

Instantly, I see flood of data scroll across the screen. I see my old social security number, my height, my date of birth, my age, the high school I attended, and many other things. All of it is personal information, and I want to know the source of such knowledge.

"How does it know all of this information about me?" I ask. I'm sure Elise and Dr. Bradshaw went through the same thing the first time they tried on the suits.

"We think it somehow has access to the old NSA files. Apparently, they are still online somewhere."

"A live feed of some kind?"

"We think so."

"What about tracking? You said your dad disabled the suits' ability to transmit location, right?"

"That was one of the first things we investigated. We certainly didn't want to risk turning this place into a homing beacon for every sentry in the area. Dad was able to identify and disable the tracking capability without too much trouble. I think he read about it in the manual."

"The manual?"

"Yes, it's a data file you can access and read in the helmet display. Dad read the entire manual one evening. He was quite a sight. He sat in a chair wearing the full suit with the helmet for several hours." Elise laughs. "He didn't even move. He looked like a statue sitting there but he was actually reading the entire time."

The flood of data scrolling across the display inside my helmet stops. And then the following message scrolls across:

... Initialization Complete ... Recognize User Adam Reese ... All Systems Online ...

And then the blue screen and the printed message on it disappears and I can now see everything around me. I look all around the room in amazement, taking it all in. I turn and look at Elise.

"The field of view is enormous," I say. "It's like I'm not even wearing anything."

"It is amazing, isn't it?"

I suddenly hear an incredibly loud screeching sound, followed by a loud gnawing sound, as if the sound of someone chewing on something has been amplified in my ears a thousand times over. I grab both sides of the helmet, placing my hands right over my ears, but it doesn't do any good. The sound is coming directly from the speakers on the inside. The sound is painful and it's almost more than I can handle. I grab the helmet and start to pull it off my head and then I remember the cable connecting it to the suit. I'm afraid of damaging anything, so I leave the helmet on and endure it.

"Adam! What's wrong?" Elise asks.

"A loud screeching sound! It sounds like it's coming from the wall!"

"The audio sensitivity must be up too high. You've got to turn it down."

"How?"

"Look into the upper right corner of the display."

I look into the upper right corner of my display and a menu drops down into my field of view.

"See it?" Elise asks.

"A menu … I see it." It's very hard to make out what Elise is saying with the painful noise filling my head.

"Look directly at the option that says audio and blink twice very quickly."

I look through the menu choices: video display, audio, distortion, and other options. I stare directly at the option that says "audio" and blink twice as fast as I can. Another menu appears and I see a list of new options that includes volume, sensitivity, and some others.

"I have a new menu," I say.

"Okay, now select sensitivity the same way."

I stare directly at the option that says "sensitivity" and blink twice quickly. The display now reads "sensitivity," and I see that it is set as high as it will go.

"It says one hundred percent sensitivity," I say.

"Okay, say: make sensitivity twenty five percent."

I repeat the phrase into the helmet and instantly the loud screeching and gnawing sounds disappear. I take in a deep breath and slowly release it. My ears are now hurting and I suspect it'll take a while for the pain to stop.

"What was that all about?" I ask.

"Sensitivity is used to hear things in other rooms and from far away," Elise says. "For some reason, the suit thought you wanted to hear the rats in the wall and it turned up the volume for you."

"Will something like that happen again?"

"Unlikely. The suit will remember your settings going forward. How does it feel?"

"A little tight in the crotch."

Elise laughs. "Take a few steps," she says. "Walk to me."

I carefully and slowly take a few steps in front of me. Even though I can see everything clearly, for some reason I feel a little off balance. I am suddenly overcome with an incredible feeling of vertigo and fall down, catching myself with my hands on the ground in front of me.

"Don't worry," Elise says. "It's normal to feel a little disoriented at first. It'll quickly pass.

I slowly stand up, pause for a moment and look around the room to get my bearings. Elise was right. The vertigo I felt just a moment ago has now passed and I'm feeling much better now … much more confident. I take a few careful steps toward Elise.

"There," she says. "You're getting it. Now, walk a little more."

I turn around and walk to the opposite end of the room. Everything is starting to feel more natural, and I'm walking more quickly now.

"Good," Elise says. "Now, walk to me again, except a little faster this time."

I turn around and walk over to Elise, moving my feet a little more quickly.

"Again," Elise says. "Faster."

I turn and run with everything in me to the end of the room, turn around, and run back. I do this several times, reversing course each time I reach a wall.

"Okay, speedy," Elise says. "I think you've got it."

I slow my sprint to a slow jog and then stop altogether. I'm breathing heavily now and take a moment to catch my breath.

"Okay," Elise says. "The last thing we're going to go over is invisibility. Now we get to the fun stuff."

"Do I access it through the menu?" I ask.

"You can, but it's much easier to use the controls on your wrist."

I look down at both of my hands and see what appears to be a control pad of some sort on my left wrist. I didn't even notice it earlier. It looks like a digital watch that's built into the suit. With my right hand, I scroll through an abbreviated menu on the little control pad and see an option that says "stealth."

"Stealth?" I ask.

"That's the one."

I select stealth on the tiny control panel and the display now reads "stealth engaged." In the upper left corner of my visor, I see a red indicator light next to the stealth option.

I look down at my hands. I still see them. I then look down at my legs and feet. They are still there, although they do look a little blurry, almost like I could use a good pair of reading glasses to correct the fuzziness around them.

"It's not working," I say.

"Oh, yes it is!"

"But my hands and my feet … I can still see them."

"That's because they are close to your eyes. The invisibility only works when you are a few feet away from someone wearing the suit."

"Are you sure?"

"I can't see you right now."

I look up at Elise. I see her very clearly and she is several feet away from me. Still, I have my doubts, especially if I'm going to be wearing this thing out in public. With our lives on the line, there's no room for failure.

"I don't know," I say.

"Well, I do. Come with me into the hallway and see if you can see your reflection in the window."

Elise walks to the door and then pauses and looks back at me. "What are you waiting for?"

I follow her into the dimly-lit hallway and stand right next to her in front of a window that has been boarded up from the outside. I look into the dirty window and can barely make out Elise's reflection, but not my own. I hold my hand up in front of my face and can clearly see it through my visor, but I see nothing in the window. I wave my hand back and forth in the air ... nothing. So, it's true ... I am indeed invisible and this is what it feels like. Interesting.

"Nice," I say.

"See? Told ya."

"You sure did!"

Elise pats me on the back. "You can take the suit off for a while. Let's grab a bite to eat. We have to have something in our stomachs if we're going to be of any use today."

"That's it? That's everything I need to know about the suit?"

"No, but we've covered all of the major things you'll need. You'll pick up on more of the suit's capabilities and feature as you go. It's very intuitive. I pick up on new things it can do all the time."

"C'mon," Elise says as she starts walking down the hallway. "Let's go; I'm hungry." She turns a corner in the hallway and disappears.

CHAPTER 5

I QUICKLY TAKE THE SUIT OFF and return it to the rack it was hanging on earlier. I place the helmet on the shelf next to the other one. For a moment, I think about all of the abuse my family and I and all of the people around us have suffered at the hands of those wearing suits such as these. I think of all the ruined lives and shattered families at the hands of the sentries, and I feel anger build inside me, like a pot of water coming to a slow boil. And then I realize that without the suits that give them their special abilities, the sentries are just people … human beings just like me who can be defeated … *will* be defeated, if I have any say in the matter.

I hear a low growling sound emanating from my belly. I'm hungry. Grabbing a little something to eat does sound very appealing right now. I leave the room and start walking down the hallway in the direction I saw Elise go a moment ago. It suddenly occurs to me that I have no idea where in this large building she went to. I keep walking and eventually I hear the faint sound of voices up ahead. I continue walking toward the voices until I locate the source.

I come to an open door with a faint light emanating from within. I walk over to it, look inside, and see Elise, Dr. Bradshaw, Maggie, and a few other people I don't recognize. They are all gathered around a small table. I walk in and every head in the room turns my way, but no one says anything. Elise smiles at me and I return the smile. She pulls out a chair beside her and pats her hand on the seat, an invitation to sit next to her. It's an invitation I'm all too happy to accept. I walk over to the empty chair and sit down and everyone returns their attention to Dr. Bradshaw, who I apparently interrupted.

Dr. Bradshaw and Maggie are sitting right next to each other and they are both turned sideways in their chairs, facing each other.

"Not all things are as they appear," Dr. Bradshaw says to Maggie as he looks straight into her eyes. Maggie says nothing in reply. She just stares back, wide-eyed.

Dr. Bradshaw holds one of his empty hands out to her. He then holds it up in the air and shows his hand to everyone in the room. He brings his hand down in front of Maggie, makes a tight fist, and then slowly opens his hand again, revealing a quarter.

"How did you do that?" Maggie asks in amazement.

"Shhh …" Dr. Bradshaw says. "It requires complete silence to reach into the beyond and pull things into the here and now."

I feel Elise's elbow hit me in my ribs and I look over to her.

"He's really hamming it up," she whispers. "He used to do magic tricks for me like this all the time when I was a kid." Elise smiles, shakes her head, and then rolls her eyes.

Dr. Bradshaw closes his hand around the quarter again, puts both hands behind his back, and then holds both of his clenched fists out in front of him.

"Which hand is the coin in?" he asks Maggie.

Maggie reaches out and taps one of the clenched fists. "This one," she says.

Dr. Bradshaw slowly opens the clenched fist Maggie selected and holds his empty palm out so everyone can see it.

"It's got to be in the other hand then," Maggie says.

Dr. Bradshaw slowly opens his other clenched hand. It's empty, too.

"You've got to watch him, Maggie," Elise says. "He's a shark."

"Where is it?" Maggie asks with a look of exasperation.

"It was with you all along," Dr. Bradshaw says as he reaches behind one of Maggie's ears, pretends to grab something, and then slowly brings his open hand back out with the coin in it.

"Nuh-uh!" Maggie says. "You were hiding it in your hand the whole time!"

"Ah, smart girl!" Dr. Bradshaw says as he pats Maggie's shoulder. "Very smart, indeed."

Dr. Bradshaw turns around in his chair and faces the table. "What do you think, Adam?" he asks. "About the suit."

"Piece of cake," I say. "I'm ready."

"He's already a pro," Elise adds.

"Good," Dr. Bradshaw says. "I knew you would catch on quickly."

A door on the opposite end of the room opens and a young woman I don't recognize walks in carrying a box. A man follows behind her, carrying a tray of cups. The two walk around the room and hand an apple and a cup of water to each person.

I pick up the golden apple and stare at it in amazement. I can't even imagine where it came from. "I haven't seen one of these in years," I say.

"Connections, Adam," Dr. Bradshaw says. "It pays to have friends in low places." Dr. Bradshaw smiles with a look of satisfaction.

"What is it?" Maggie asks. It suddenly occurs to me that she is probably too young to have any memory of apples, or any other fruit, for that matter.

"It's an apple. You eat it … like this." I take a bite of my apple to show Maggie how to eat the foreign fruit and I am unprepared for the incredible sweet taste that greets me. I can't even remember the last time I've eaten any fruit and I am almost overwhelmed by the intensity of sugary sweetness. I chew very slowly, enjoying every last second of it.

"Now you try it," I say. "Take a bite of yours."

Maggie awkwardly brings the fruit up to her mouth with both hands, as if she's not even sure how to hold it. She takes a small, cautious bite, and chews slowly. And then I see her eyes slowly grow wide. I've seen this look on her before, when I gave her the chocolate food bar. It's a look of new discovery and of pure joy. I don't think I will ever grow tired of seeing it.

"Mmmm!" she says.

"There's a whole world of great foods I've got to introduce you to," I say. Maggie just looks at me without saying anything and takes another bite, a bite that is almost too large for her mouth.

Dr. Bradshaw clears his throat. "Okay," he says. "Let's go over the plan one last time."

"I think I've got it down by now," Elise says.

"You can never be too prepared," Dr. Bradshaw says with his half-chewed apple in one hand.

"I'd like to go over it again," I say.

"Very good," Dr. Bradshaw says. "The plan is simple. Adam and Elise … you will leave here, wearing the two captured sentry suits in our possession. You will each be armed with a bowie knife. You will then walk to the old train depot, which isn't far from here, and wait for the two sentries that patrol that area to make their midday patrols. When the sentries appear and start harassing the locals, which they are sure to do, you sneak up behind them and slit their throats. Jackson, Riggs, Walker, and Perez will follow you to the depot. They will be dressed in plain clothes, of course, to blend in with the crowd. After you take care of the sentries, they will be in charge of stripping them of their suits and bringing the suits back here. You are not to assist them. The suits you are wearing are too valuable. Your primary objective at that point is to return to our base of operations undetected. Any questions?"

"None; I'm ready," Elise says.

"Adam?"

"It's a simple enough plan and I think it has a strong chance of success …" I pause and look down at the floor beside me as my thoughts turn to Mom and Sarah. I've got to reach them and Dr. Bradshaw has got to understand that.

Dr. Bradshaw leans forward in his chair. "But?" he asks.

"I've got to reach my family and let them know I'm okay. My home isn't far from the old train depot. With the suit, I can safely reach them and —"

"Out of the question," Dr. Bradshaw says with a raised hand. "It's much too dangerous, Adam, even with the suit. You must not forget that you're a wanted man."

"But if I —"

"They'll be looking for you there, Adam. No, you can't go there again. We can find a way to send a message to your family, but you must not have any direct contact with them."

I say nothing in reply and look down at the table in front of me.

"Very well, then," Dr. Bradshaw says. "The time for action is upon us. Elise, Adam, if you'll go ahead and suit up, I'll make sure Jackson, Riggs, Walker, and Perez are ready to follow you."

My apple is little more than a core at this point. I've been nibbling on it so much that I've chewed into the area that holds the seeds. It was delicious, and I'll be holding on to the experience for a long time in my mind. In the days and weeks ahead when I'm hungry and I don't have anything to eat, I'll be thinking about that apple. I quickly finish my glass of water as everyone around me stands and leaves the room.

Elise follows the crowd out the door and I follow closely behind her. Maggie walks out behind me, still holding her half-eaten apple, still enjoying every single bite.

CHAPTER 6

ELISE AND I BOTH PUT THE sentry suits on again over the clothes we are wearing. Maggie sits in a corner of the room and watches, still eating her apple. I wouldn't be surprised at all if she's still eating that apple when we return after completing our mission.

I see Elise pick up a bowie knife from the shelf the helmets are on and strap it to her thigh. I don't recall seeing them there earlier. I pick up the other knife, strap it to my leg, and then grab my helmet.

"Are you ready to do this?" Elise asks with her helmet in her hand. I detect a bit of apprehension in her voice, as if she's not really asking me if I'm ready so much as she is looking for confirmation that we're doing the right thing.

"As ready as I'm ever going to be," I say.

Elise tries to smile, but it looks forced. "Okay, let's do it," she says.

Elise walks out of the room and I follow behind her, with Maggie following right behind me. Elise knows how to navigate this large building much better than I do, so I let her lead the way.

As the three of us walk down the dim corridor, I can't help but feel like I'm walking to a funeral, perhaps my own. The mood is somber and no one speaks. We go from one hallway to the next in what feels like a labyrinth that even the best lab rat would get hopelessly lost in. We turn another corner and I finally see rays of light piercing the boarded-up windows of the main entrance.

As I get closer to the entrance, I see a small crowd of people gathered near the door. They are lined up in single file along the walls of the hallway, leaving a large empty space between them for us to walk through. I recognize a few faces from Dr. Bradshaw's meeting I attended the other day, while others are faces I've never seen before.

"Who are they?" I ask.

"People who believe in what we're about to do," Elise says. "They are people who are tired of dealing with the harassment from the sentries, and of having to pay tribute to an unknown, unseen king. They are people who are quietly, but diligently, working behind the scenes to help our cause. They are us and we are them."

We continue walking toward the crowd of people. All heads are turned toward us. All eyes are on us as we approach. We arrive at the crowd, and the first person in line reaches out and touches Elise's shoulder. "Resistance!" he says as we continue walking toward the door. One by one each person in the crowd reaches out and does the same. Each person touches either our arm or our shoulder; each person says, "Resistance."

We reach the door leading out and Dr. Bradshaw is there to send us off. "You're ready for this," he says. "It's a solid plan and you've got the best equipment."

Elise gives her dad a big hug. "I'll see you shortly," she says.

I look behind me and see Maggie right at my feet. She's looking up to me as though she expects to go with us. I kneel down on one knee in front of her, place my helmet on the ground beside me, and put a hand on her shoulder.

"Maggie, I have a very important job for you to do while I'm gone. I can count on you, can't I?"

"Uh-huh," she says while nodding her head.

"Here's what I want you to do. I need someone to watch over Dr. Bradshaw while we're gone, to make sure he's okay. I don't think his health is all that good."

I look up at Dr. Bradshaw and wink at him. He quickly picks up on what I'm trying to do and he coughs a couple of times, as though he's not feeling well. "Yes," Dr. Bradshaw says. "I have been feeling a bit under the weather lately."

I look back down at Maggie. "You'll watch over him for me, won't you?"

"I can do it," Maggie says. "I'll take care of him until you get back." Maggie runs up to me, gives me a quick hug, and then darts over to Dr. Bradshaw's side.

I pick my helmet up off the ground and stand up again. I turn and look into Elise's eyes and nod. She nods back. We're as ready as we're ever going to be.

Elise puts her helmet on and connects her data and power cable dangling from the suit. I pick my helmet up and pause just before I lift it up to my head. I remember the problem I had with the audio sensitivity earlier and can't help but wonder if I'll have a repeat of the experience, or if it will truly remember my settings, as Elise said. I slowly lower the helmet over my head and connect the data and power cable. Instantly, I see a message scroll across the screen:

... Recognize User Adam Reese ... All Systems Online ...

The message disappears as quickly as it appeared and I am able to see clearly through the visor. The helmet appears to have remembered my settings.

"Ready?" I hear Elise ask through the speaker in my helmet.

"Let's do it," I say back to her.

Elise reaches down to the control panel on her wrist, and then she quickly fades away.

I reach down to the control panel on my wrist, select stealth, and see an indicator light appear in my visor next to stealth mode. I look down at my hands and feet. I still see them. I'll have to learn to trust the suit when it tells me I'm invisible. It's going to take a little time for me to get used to this.

I see the door open and realize Elise just walked out. I follow right behind her.

"Give 'em hell!" I hear someone in the crowd of people behind me say.

I walk out of the building and step into a mission that will forever change the dynamic between the sentries and the outlanders. I have an unexplained uneasiness about the whole thing gnawing at me from within. There's no turning back now.

CHAPTER 7

A BLAST OF COLD AIR HITS ME as I walk out of our safe haven. I didn't expect this and the clothes I'm wearing underneath the sentry suit don't exactly provide much in the way of insulation. And I also just discovered the hard way that the suit doesn't act as a windbreaker, either. The cold air is cutting right through the suit and I'm feeling every bit of it. I'll definitely remember to dress for the weather next time … if there is a next time.

I start walking toward the train depot, following the sound of Elise's faint footsteps as I go. Occasionally, I get close to her as I'm walking and I can see her just a little bit.

"Are you with me?" Elise asks.

"Right behind you," I say as I try to be careful not to walk into her. It's apparent that this business of walking around invisible is just as much an art as it is a skill. I may have the basics down, but I've still got a lot to learn.

It suddenly occurs to me that we are communicating by radio and I have no idea whether our transmission can be picked up by anyone other than us.

"Are our radio transmissions secure?" I ask. "What's keeping the other sentries from listening in on us?"

"They are secure. That's one of the first things Dad worked on when we got the suits. Ordinarily, our radio transmission would be open to any sentries in the area, but Dad scrambled them so that only we can hear each other."

Elise I and continue walking toward our destination. As we walk, I see Jackson, Riggs, Walker, and Perez walk past us on their way. I have no idea who these guys are or where they came from, but I'm glad they are on our side. They don't look like guys I'd want to have upset with me, that's for sure. They look highly conditioned, as though they have always had plenty to eat and they work out on a regular basis. They each have shaved heads and no facial hair, and they are dressed in regular street clothes to blend in. I can't help but wonder why these tough-looking guys aren't doing the job that Elise and I are getting ready to do. Why not them instead of us?

"Adam?" Elise says. Her soft voice breaks my thoughts and brings me back to the here and now.

"Yes?"

"I can hear your footsteps as you walk."

I am suddenly aware of the loud sounds my feet are making as I kick up gravels as I walk. I may be invisible to anyone around me but I wouldn't exactly call myself stealthy.

"Try to walk softly, Adam, like you're walking on clouds."

"Got it. Stealthy feet."

I try to imagine that I am a cat that is stealthily stalking its prey, which isn't too far from the truth. I carefully and quietly place each foot in front of the other, being extra careful not to kick the gravel.

"Much better," Elise says.

We continue walking, and I can see the old train depot not far in the distance. It's a place that has served countless people in years past, a gateway to various places all around the United States and Canada. But now it only serves as a common place for people to trade what few goods they have. The depot's awnings protect people from the elements. Its tracks are now abandoned, save for a few old passenger cars that have long ago had their windows smashed out. Their interiors are probably covered in mold and mildew these days, and they are probably also home to a variety of little furry critters. I doubt they are a place a person would want to hang out in.

"Adam?" Elise asks as we continue walking to our destination.

"Yes?"

"What's it like?"

I'm not sure what she's referring to, and I pause for a moment before responding. "What do you mean?"

"Killing someone. What's it like?"

I suddenly realize that she has never had to take a life to survive after the eruption of Yellowstone. I can only assume that Dr. Bradshaw shielded her from such things. She's lucky, that's for sure. The sentry I killed the other day wasn't the first life I've taken, but I've never taken a life without a very good reason. It's always been a last resort for me ... a matter of survival. If it was up to me, we'd all be living in harmony together singing Kumbaya under a rainbow, but it's not up to me. If it is, I didn't get the memo.

"It's hard to put into words," I say. "It's not really something you can describe. You just do what you've got to do and then try to put it behind you. Let's just say it's something I never want to become comfortable with."

"I've been telling myself that I can do this over and over again ever since we started walking here. I'm starting to have some doubts, Adam."

I say nothing in reply. She's an incredibly strong person and I am confident that she has the ability to do what's necessary when the time comes.

We arrive at the train depot. Jackson, Riggs, Walker, and Perez have already taken positions around the perimeter, blending in with the few people who are here. I crouch down between two old train cars. I'm not sure where Elise is.

"Where are you?" I ask.

"Between the two older passenger cars closest to the terminal."

I realize that's exactly where I am.

"Where are you?" Elise asks.

I reach out all around me and feel Elise's arm. I feel her pull away very quickly. "Right beside you," I say.

"You scared me!"

"Sorry."

I can imagine the fun a prankster could have with a suit like this. I can easily see someone wearing one in one of those haunted houses that used to be in Everytown, USA, every Halloween and sneaking up to and scaring the daylights out of people. The possibilities are endless.

"We shouldn't have to wait too long," Elise says. "The sentries tend to keep a tight schedule."

"Yeah, they harass people in one area for a few minutes and then move on to harass others in other areas. You can almost set your watch by them."

"At least they're consistent."

Elise and I stay in our position between the two old train cars for several minutes, waiting for a pair of sentries to reveal themselves. Neither of us says anything as we wait and watch. Jackson, Riggs, Walker, and Perez change positions and pretend to haggle with vendors, but they don't leave the area. They look like they are growing restless, just as I am.

I see two young boys playing in the distance and, for a moment, I am reminded of my carefree days as a young boy. I remember hanging out with my friends during the summer and spending many lazy days goofing off without so much as a care in the world. I watch as the two boys run back and forth. I see one boy tag the other and then the person being chased suddenly becomes the one doing the chasing.

The two boys eventually grow tired of running. Even young boys can only run so much before they run out of steam. But that doesn't necessarily mean they are done playing. I see one of the boys make the shape of a gun out of his fingers and thumb and then pretend to shoot someone walking by. The other boy does the same.

And then it hits me, like a sudden revelation or some sort of deja vu. I've seen these two boys before. These are the same two boys who were taunting me the other day, just before I killed the sentry who was harassing Elise. Yes, it's them all right; I'm sure of it. And I strongly suspect they are up to no good.

"I'll be right back," I say. "I'm going to check on something."

"Where are you going? What's wrong?"

"Nothing's wrong. I'm not going far. I'll just be a moment."

"Okay, just be careful."

"Will do."

I stand from my crouched position and start walking toward the two boys. I have no idea what I'm going to do when I get to them. For some reason, I just feel like this is something I need to do, and that I'm probably the only person who can take care of it.

I get closer to the two boys and I can now hear what they are saying. They appear to be giving an old man who is walking by them a really hard time.

"Give us something to eat!" one of the boys says to him.

"I don't have anything," the old man says as he slowly shuffles away from them.

"You're lying!" the other boy says.

"Leave me alone," the old man pleads. "I told you I don't have anything."

"Liar, liar, pants on fire!" one of the boys says.

The other boy looks at him. "Pants on fire," he repeats. The two boys nod at each other and one of them pulls a can of some kind out of his jacket pocket. The boy walks up to the man and starts squirting some sort of liquid from the can onto the man's legs. The man tries to get away, but he's too slow. He looks very old and he's having trouble walking. The boy continues squirting the liquid on the man's legs until they are very soaked.

The boy stops. I don't know if he just ran out of the liquid or if he has determined that the man is sufficiently soaked. It doesn't matter. The other boy pulls an old metal lighter out of his pocket and lights it.

"Empty your pockets, old man, or I'm going to warm things up for you!"

And then I realize what the boys are about to do. "Pants on fire," they said. These little shits just squirted lighter fluid on the old man's legs and are now threatening to set him on fire if he doesn't give them everything he has. I've seen enough.

I quietly walk right up behind the boys and switch my audio from radio to speaker. I see another setting I've never noticed before that says audio distortion. I set the distortion as high as it will go and then disengage stealth.

"Both of you!" I say. "Don't move!" My voice sounds very deep and highly distorted, like some kind of evil robot.

The two boys quickly turn around and the look on their faces changes to one of pure horror. The boy holding the lighter drops it on the ground, extinguishing the flame. I look up at the old man and see a look of fear on his face, too.

"I know what you've been doing, and I don't like it one bit!" I say to the boys. I point to one of them. "You. What's your name?"

"J-J-Jacob," the boys says.

I point to the other boy. "And you. What's your name?"

"Andrew," he says.

"Jacob and Andrew," I say. "Two troublemakers. I suppose you think what you're doing is funny? Harassing people for your own amusement?"

The two boys shake their heads no vigorously.

"Well, it's not funny. I don't want to ever see or hear of either of you harassing anyone ever again. Do you understand?"

Both boys nod their heads, their eyes are as wide as saucers.

"In fact, I'm going to be watching your every move, and if I see either of you—"

"Adam?" I hear Elise say in the speaker in my helmet. "Where are you? They're here!"

I quickly switch back to radio mode.

"On my way!" I say.

I turn and start to walk away from the two boys, take a few steps, and then stop. This situation is too ripe and I just can't help myself. I have to get in one more good scare to put an end to these kids' shenanigans forever.

I slowly turn back around to face the two boys one last time. They both look like they've just seen a ghost. Jacob's crotch is soaked and he has obviously just peed on himself. Andrew has tears streaming down his face. The old man is still standing in the same spot, too. I switch the audio back to speaker.

"You," I say as I point to the old man. "You can go." The old man turns around and shuffles off, his pants still soaked in lighter fluid.

I turn my attention back to the boys. "Remember," I say in my heavily distorted voice. "I'll be watching."

Both boys nod their heads vigorously, like a pair of bobbleheads.

Feeling satisfied, I start to turn around and head back to Elise, but once again I stop. Giving these boys a little taste of their own medicine is way too much fun, and I could easily do it all day long. *Just once more*, I think. The more I scare them, the less likely they are to give anyone a hard time again.

I turn and face the boys again and point a finger at them.

"One more thing," I say to them. And then my mind goes blank. I can't think of anything else to say to them. I don't have any more time to spare and I say the first thing that comes to mind.

"Don't do drugs!"

Both boys shake their heads as hard as they can. I turn and walk away from them, this time for good, and I hear both of them break out crying loudly behind me.

I quickly engage stealth mode and then switch my audio setting back to radio.

"Adam!" Elise says. "Where are you? They're almost in perfect position!"

"Be there in a sec."

"We may not have a sec."

I move as quickly as I can without making too much noise, but I'm not sure if it's going to be fast enough.

CHAPTER 8

AS I APPROACH THE AREA AROUND the old train depot where I left Elise earlier, I see two fully-exposed sentries talking to a man I don't recognize. I can't hear the conversation they are having, but I don't need to. I can easily tell by the look on the man's face and his reaction to what the sentries are saying to him that the conversation isn't going well. Several times, I see the sentries say something to him and then he shakes his head. They are harassing him, accusing him of something, and he's denying it. I fear this won't end well.

"I'm back," I say.

"Do you see what I see?" Elise asks.

"Sure do. Think we can get them before they decide to do something to that poor guy?"

"We can try. I don't know if we can make it in time, though."

One of the sentries takes the police baton he's carrying and strikes the man hard in the side of the head. He then shoves the man's chest, causing him to fall to the ground. The other sentry raises his police baton over his head and strikes the fallen man's body, hard. The two sentries pummel the fallen man, delivering blow after blow to his body. It's very clear that he won't last long if we don't intervene.

I start running toward the sentries. "I'll take the tall one," I say.

"The other one is mine," Elise says.

I reach down and grab the large bowie knife that's strapped to my leg, unstrap it, and pull it out of its sheath. I run toward the tall sentry as fast as I can. This time, I'm not the least bit worried about how much noise I'm making. I leap over some debris and land just behind the two sentries. The tall sentry raises his baton high over his head to strike the man one more time. I grab his arm mid-swing with my free hand, reach in front of him with my knife, and run my blade swiftly across his throat. I feel the man's body tense up, and then it goes limp and falls to the ground. One sentry down, one to go.

I look over at the other sentry, fully expecting to see it lying on the ground in a pool of its own blood, but that's not what I see. I see the sentry frantically looking all around him, as if he's desperately trying to figure out what just happened. I see him reach for the rifle that's slung across his back.

"Adam! I can't do it!" Elise says. "I just can't do it!"

I now know exactly what's going on, but there's no time to talk about it. I'll have to deal with the situation at hand first.

The sentry swings his rifle around in front of him and fires several rounds in my direction, narrowly missing me. Startled, I take a couple of steps back, and, without thinking, I put my foot down hard on the gravel beneath me to regain my footing. I see the sentry look down at my feet and then take aim right above where he just saw the gravel being disturbed. And then ... he shoots straight into my chest. In an instant, the breath in my lungs is knocked out of me and my entire body is knocked to the ground. The armor in the suit I'm wearing may have prevented the bullet from penetrating my body, but I definitely still felt its impact.

For a moment, I stare into the sky above me. The hit I just took knocked more than my breath out of me; it also knocked my sense of who I am and what I'm doing out of me, too. I suck in a deep breath of air and look up at the sentry in front of me, and then everything suddenly comes back to me like some sort of bad dream suddenly made real. *Get up, Adam!* I tell myself.

The sentry looks confused, as though he's uncertain as to whether he just killed his invisible nemesis or whether he should flee. I see him waving his rifle all around him, as though he doesn't know what to point it at. I force myself to sit up. As I do, I see the sentry look right at me. My movement must have shifted the gravel beneath me. I brace for the impact of another bullet. Instead of firing his rifle at me again, however, the sentry turns around and starts running.

I leap up from the ground, my knife still in my hand, and start running after the sentry as fast and hard as I can. He still hasn't gone into stealth mode yet. He's probably so rattled by what just happened that he isn't thinking straight. That's what I'm hoping for, anyway. If he engages stealth, I'll lose him for sure.

"Adam!" I hear Elise say in my helmet.

"I'm okay," I say. "I'm going after him."

"I'm so sorry!"

I'm breathing much too hard now to respond to her and I have to concentrate on the task at hand.

The sentry runs at a fast pace along the train tracks. It's a poor choice, since it will take him out into the open and there's essentially nowhere for him to hide now. I'm running as fast as I can but he's just a little bit faster.

My lungs are now burning and the helmet I'm wearing feels stifling. I want with everything in me to pull it off so I can take in some fresh air, but such a thing isn't possible. The sentry continues running fast and he occasionally looks behind him. He knows he's being chased. He can probably hear my footsteps behind him as I run with everything in me.

The sentry reaches up to his helmet as he's running and pulls it off, no doubt to breathe better. He tosses it on the ground and continues running, still looking behind him as he tries to catch a glimpse of his pursuer. I realize now that I'm not going to be able to catch him. He's faster than me, and he's now running without a helmet to impede his breathing, a luxury I can't afford at the moment. I bring my run to a slow jog and then just as I'm about to come to a full stop, something I didn't see coming and certainly didn't expect happens.

As the sentry continues to run from me, I see him turn and look behind him once more. And then I see his feet slip beneath him, as if he just walked through a slick spot in the road, or perhaps the gravel was too deep in that particular area. Whatever the cause, his feet fly out from beneath him and he lands hard on the ground in front of him.

I run over to him and jump on his back, driving one of my knees into his lower back to pin him down. I grab his hair with my free hand and pull his head back hard. I place the blade of my bowie knife against his neck, ready to put an end to all of the misery I'm sure he's caused in his life … and then I realize he's unconscious. He must have hit his head hard on the gravel beneath him when he went down. He's gasping for breath and a thick line of drool is hanging from his mouth.

I pause with the knife at his throat. The goal of this operation is to get the suit, not necessarily to kill anyone. The killing part was only deemed necessary to get the suit. I don't think anyone could have predicted that something like this would have happened. I could strip him of the suit and just leave him here. I'm sure he'll make his way back inside the wall somehow. His comrades will probably make fun of him, and maybe he'll be demoted, but at least he'll get to live. And then I remember what this man did just a moment ago. I see him beating that poor man with his police baton in my mind. If I hadn't stopped him, he would have killed that man for sure. The man lying on the ground beneath me is a killer, and he'll kill again if I don't put an end to his ability to harm others in the future.

I run my knife across his neck. His body tries to take in a few extra breaths of air, but it's no use. He makes a loud gurgling sound … and then all movement ceases.

The sentry is dead.

CHAPTER 9

I STAND, TAKE MY HELMET OFF, and take in as much of the cold, fresh air as my lungs can hold. There's a faint beeping sound coming from my helmet. I look inside and can barely make out the word "stealth" on the display. I look down at my wrist control and realize I am no longer invisible. Removing the helmet must automatically disengage stealth.

I hear footsteps running toward me in the distance. I look behind me to see who's pursuing me and I see Walker and Perez approaching.

"Nice work, Reese," Perez says as he approaches with the sentry's helmet in his hands. Walker and Perez run up to the dead sentry and immediately start removing the suit off of his body.

"Where's Elise?" I ask.

"She's on her way back to the base," Walker says as he pulls the top half of the suit off of the man's lifeless body. "She followed right behind Jackson and Riggs when they picked up the first suit."

I watch Walker and Perez strip the suit off the man's dead body as I catch my breath. They are methodical and they work fast. In nearly no time at all, the suit is free of its former wearer, a man who is dressed very well. I can't help but wonder if everyone living inside the wall has the resources to dress as well as this man does.

"Let's get out of here," Walker says. "It won't take long before your handiwork is discovered by the other sentries. We don't want to be here when that happens."

I turn around and start to bring my helmet up to my head again when I see several people approaching in the distance. I recognize them. They are the people who were trading back at the train depot when I went after the sentry attacking the man just moments ago. As they approach, I see that they look intensely curious. Can't blame them, I guess. It's not like seeing a pair of sentries go down is an everyday occurrence.

Walker, Perez, and I walk toward the crowd. Going through them is the quickest way to get back to our base of operations. As I get closer to the crowd, I recognize the man who was being beaten by the sentries just moments ago. He's hobbling, and he has both of his arms wrapped firmly around his belly, as if he's protecting an injury. His face is covered in blood from the blow he took to the head. I start to put my helmet back on and then I see the man looking at me and walking toward me. I lower my helmet and walk over to him.

"Reese, we need to get out of here," Perez says.

"I'll just be a moment," I say.

Walker and Perez keep walking through the crowd.

The man with the bloody head walks up to me. "Thank you," he says.

I nod to him but say nothing. The crowd is moving in closer.

"Who are you?" another man asks.

"Who I am isn't important," I say. "But what I represent is."

"You're Adam Reese, aren't you?" a woman asks.

I don't answer her. The crowd is growing even larger and they are starting to surround me. There appears to be more people here now than there was earlier. Where are they coming from? I don't know, but apparently the word that something big just happened is spreading fast.

I hear my name mentioned several times around me. "It's Adam Reese," one man says to another man. "He killed that sentry with his bare hands," a woman says. "He's a one-man army," another man says. This is getting ridiculous. If this keeps up, they'll have me flying through the air and shooting lightning bolts from my eyes before it's over with.

"I'm just a simple man who's tired of all of the abuse at the hands of the sentries," I say. "Aren't all of you tired, too?" No one says anything. They all have blank expressions on their faces. "You only need to know that I am part of the resistance against King Darius and his army of sentry soldiers that have been making all our lives miserable for far too long."

"You're just one man," another man in the crowd says. "How can you possibly win against the king's army?"

"You only see one man before you," I say, "but I can assure you, there are many more of us working in the shadows to put an end to the tyranny. If we all join together, we have a much stronger chance of winning back our lives … and our freedom."

"And what if we don't?" another woman asks.

"You are all free to choose your own destinies," I say. "There is no compulsion to join us, but do keep in mind that there is strength in numbers."

I see two young boys making their way through the crowd and realize they are the two boys I was talking to earlier. The boy who peed on himself still has a dark wet spot on his pants, although he doesn't seem to mind. The boys move to the front of the crowd and stare at me in awe, as though I'm some sort of celebrity.

"Adam? Where are you?" I hear the faint sound of Elise's voice coming from the inside of my helmet. I quickly put the helmet on my head and connect the cable.

"I'm here. What's wrong?"

"Nothing, we just haven't heard from you. I was a little … a little concerned. Everyone's back except you."

I realize that I've been lingering here for far too long. I don't see Walker and Perez anywhere. I'm surprised they've already made it back.

"Nothing's wrong," I say. "I'm on my way."

I quickly select stealth mode and disappear from the crowd's view. I start walking through them, being careful to walk as quietly as possible. I hear them talking about me as I walk. They are a crowd of mixed emotions. Some of them seem to be very enthusiastic about the idea of joining the resistance and fighting back, while others express skepticism.

I reach the end of the crowd, or the beginning. It all depends on a person's perspective, I suppose. I pause and look back at them once more. I wonder if they understand the magnitude of inaction … of doing nothing. I wonder if they even realize how powerful a force they would be if they would just work together and fight back. I fear there's only so much the rag-tag group Dr. Bradshaw has assembled can do. But there's strength in numbers.

I see the two boys again. They have moved to the end of the crowd where I am, as if they are trying to follow me, to get in one last look. They still look as though they are in awe, as if they've just seen something truly amazing. Perhaps they have. They may have just witnessed the beginning of the outlander's awakening. Perhaps.

I turn and walk away.

CHAPTER 10

I WALK INTO OUR SAFE HAVEN, being careful to make sure that no one is around to watch me open the door. Even though I'm not visible, a door that suddenly opens and closes on its own would certainly be suspicious to anyone who isn't privy to our operations. I can't take any chances. There are few people I trust outside the inner workings of this facility. A single sighting of anything that looks out of the norm by anyone who is sympathetic to the king and his minions could draw unwanted attention to this place, and could ultimately be our undoing.

I close the door behind me and secure its simple lock. I disengage stealth mode and work quickly to remove the stifling helmet from my head. I pull the helmet off and take in a large breath of fresh air. With all its capabilities, the helmet doesn't seem to have been designed with good air exchange being a primary consideration. The display fogs up on occasion, too. I'm sure the engineers who designed the suit would've corrected these deficiencies in later models, but I doubt the company even exists any more. I'll have to learn to live with it, problems and all.

I start walking down the dim hallway, helmet in hand, although I'm not sure where I'm walking to ... toward the sound of people's voices, I suppose. I need to take the time to learn my way around this place. I don't walk very far until I hear the sound of approaching footsteps, footsteps that are quickly growing louder. Someone is running toward me and I stop in my tracks to wait and see what all the commotion is about.

In the distance, I see the faint silhouette of a person approaching, and then I see her. Elise runs up to me and grabs one of my arms. She looks as though she is consumed with worry.

"Elise, are you okay?" I ask.

"I'm so sorry!" she says. "Please forgive me, Adam! I'm so sorry!"

"Sorry for what?"

"For freezing earlier ... and for putting your life at risk when you had to chase my sentry down and do the job I should have done." Elise is now holding onto my arm with both hands, and she's squeezing hard, as if gripping me harder will somehow make it all better.

"There's nothing to forgive," I say. Elise relaxes her strained look; her grip on my arm softens. She tilts her head to one side and gives me a look that says "are you sure?"

"Let's go have a look at the fruits of our labor," I say. "Let's check out the suits we captured."

"Okay," Elise says softly.

Elise and I both walk down the hallway and I let Elise guide us as we go. She continues to hold my arm as we walk.

"I'll do better next time," Elise says as we walk. "I promise."

"Don't lose any sleep over it. Listen, this business of killing … it's never easy. It's a terrible thing, actually. It's not something you ever want to become comfortable with, that's for sure."

"Still, we're in a war now. At least, I think that's what you could call what we're involved in. I know I don't ever want to become comfortable with such a thing, but I still have to accept it as a means to secure our freedom. It's necessary."

"War is hell."

"Indeed," Elise says. "It is."

We turn a corner in the hallway and Elise leads me to a room with an open door. A faint flickering light emanates from it, no doubt from the oil lantern lighting the room within.

"They're in here," Elise says. I feel her release my arm and she walks in front of me, entering the room first. I follow closely behind.

Like nearly all of the rooms in this building, this one is also very plain. The windowless room has simple block walls, a hanging ceiling that is stained from water damage, and a tile floor that is chipped, scratched, and in desperate need of a cleaning. A single oil lantern sits on a shelf on the far end of the room. And lying on the floor are the two sentry suits Elise I and just captured. They are covered in blood around both collars. I see blood on both of the helmets, too. A young woman I don't recognize is sitting on the floor, cleaning the suits with a blood-stained rag. Several people are gathered around the suits and are looking down at them and quietly talking amongst themselves. Among them are Dr. Bradshaw and Maggie. All heads turn and gaze upon us as we enter the room.

"Adam!" Maggie says as she runs over to me carrying Carrie Anne.

"Hey, kiddo!" I say as I put an arm around her shoulder and squeeze her body in a little hug.

"Adam?" Maggie says to me in a soft voice.

I look down into her eyes. "Uh-huh?"

She motions with her finger for me to come close to her, like she has some kind of secret she wants to share with me. I lean my body down to her.

"Carrie Anne says she's really glad you're back okay," she whispers.

I give Maggie a big smile. "Well, you tell Carrie Anne that I'm very glad to come back to both of you."

Maggie smiles and her face radiates. "Okay, I'll tell her."

I stand and see Dr. Bradshaw walking over to me.

"Excellent work, Adam!" he says as he walks up to me, pats me hard on the back, and then rests his hand on my shoulder. He is practically beaming with satisfaction. I smile and give him a nod of my head, like it's all in a day's work.

"Did you encounter any problems?" Dr. Bradshaw asks. I see Elise give me a cautious look, as if she's worried I'm going to tell her father that she wasn't able to take care of her part of the plan. It's very clear that she has omitted this piece of information from her report, and I'm not about to tell her father what happened. I'll leave that up to her, if she ever decides to.

"No problems," I say. "The plan worked just as you said it would."

"Excellent," Dr. Bradshaw says. "I've been giving a little thought to the success of our first mission, and since things went so well the first time around, I believe we should go out again … today. We strike while the iron is hot."

"This evening?" I ask. I am surprised by what Dr. Bradshaw is saying. I am exhausted, and just the thought of doing what we just did all over again without getting a good night's rest doesn't appeal to me at all. I look over at Elise and the look on her face tells me that she is just as surprised as I am. "But I thought we were going to wait until—"

"Yes, that was the plan," Dr. Bradshaw interjects. "If we wait to commence with a second attack, there's a chance the sentries might suspect something. It's a small chance, but a chance nonetheless. They might be more vigilant, more careful in the days and weeks ahead. But if we strike again today, before they even have a chance to realize that any of their comrades are missing, our chances of acquiring two more suits are very strong."

Three of the people who were watching the young girl clean the suits leave the room, chatting quietly as they go. The young woman continues to scrub the blood off of one of the helmets. She is very involved with her work and doesn't even look up at us.

"Where do you suggest we go this time?" Elise asks. "The train depot is no good anymore."

"What about the area around the bearing factory?" I ask. "It's not too far and there's a lot of activity in the area with all of the dog fights."

"I believe that area would do nicely," Dr. Bradshaw says. "Elise?"

"It's a good location," Elise says. "It's as good as we could hope for."

"Then it's settled, "Dr. Bradshaw says with a look of elation. "Elise, you'll need to suit up again."

Elise looks at me. I haven't even had a chance to take my suit off. "Okay," she says, "but maybe Adam needs to take a break before we head out again. Adam, do you need any water or anything?"

"I'll get it!" Maggie says as she jumps up and darts out of the room, leaving her doll on the ground. She didn't even give me a chance to give an answer as to whether I was thirsty or not.

Elise starts walking toward the door. "Let me change into something a little more appropriate," she says as she walks out.

It looks like this is all the break we're going to get before we go back for round two. It's better to get it over with. At least I'll sleep well tonight.

I look down at the young woman still cleaning the blood off of the helmet on the ground in front of me. It's a macabre scene. Her rag is covered in blood. It's also on her clothes and on the floor around her. I didn't even realize so much blood had been spilled. It's times like these that I have to remind myself why we are involved in such a thing. *It's for freedom*, I tell myself. *So that my family and I can have a future that doesn't involve hunting for a weekly tribute or constantly having to dodge the sentries.*

My family. My thoughts turn to them and how worried they must be. I'm sure they've been questioned by the sentries, but did the sentries merely question them or did they use their tactics of persuasion and try to beat information out of them? I have no way of knowing. I am overcome with a feeling of incredible anxiety and concern for them. I've got to get to them, and the old bearing factory isn't far from home. If I could just reach them, I could let them know I'm okay. Maybe I could even bring them here where it's safe.

Maggie bursts through the door, holding a cup of water in front of her with both hands. "Here it is, Adam!" she says as she holds it up to me.

I reach down and take it from her, bring it up to my mouth, and take every last drop of it in with one large drink. The water is warm and it has a bit of an odd, earthy taste to it, but I don't care. I didn't even realize how thirsty I was. I give the empty cup back to Maggie. She places it on the floor in one corner of the room and then sits down on the floor with her doll again. There's something about Maggie playing on the floor just a few feet away from the bloody mess the young woman is cleaning up that doesn't seem entirely right to me, but it's not something I have time to address. I'm still very much consumed with thoughts of reaching my family.

"The bearing factory," I say to Dr. Bradshaw. "That's not far from my home. Perhaps I could check in on Mom and Sarah since I'll be so close to them. Just a couple of minutes is all I'll need. With the suit, I could sneak in undetected and—"

"Out of the question," Dr. Bradshaw says while holding one hand up in the air.

"If I could reach them, I could bring them here and—"

"It's much too dangerous, Adam. You must never forget that you are a wanted man with a high price on your head. No, it's simply out of the question. There are too many unforeseen consequences to what you are proposing.

"Ready for action," I hear behind me. I turn around and see Elise standing in the doorway, wearing her sentry suit again, her helmet tucked in under one of her arms.

"Let's make it happen," I say as I turn and walk toward the door. There's no use arguing with Dr. Bradshaw about reaching Mom and Sarah. It's clear that he's strongly opposed to the idea. Still, my thoughts of Mom and Sarah are going to weigh heavily on me in the coming days and weeks. It's not like I can just forget about them with the knowledge that they have no idea what happened to me. At this point, all they know is that I left the house a couple of days ago and never came home. I'm sure they are heavily burdened by it, just as the knowledge that I'll be so close to them and unable to contact them will weigh heavily on me.

"I'll get your cleanup crew assembled again," Dr. Bradshaw says.

"Do you think they'll be up for it so soon?" I ask as I pause beside Elise at the door.

"I don't even have to ask," Dr. Bradshaw says as he walks toward the door. "I know they'll be up for it. They're former Marines. Those guys are always ready for action." Dr. Bradshaw leaves the room.

I hear Maggie make a noise of some kind as she plays with her doll. She seems to be obsessed with that doll, as if she's in another world most of the time. Perhaps it's her way of escaping the crazy world around her. Can't say that I blame her. Sometimes I wish I could do the same.

I feel a hand take hold of my free hand and realize that it's Elise. I squeeze her hand back and for a moment we stand together, hand in hand. I turn my head and look at her and see that she is already looking at me.

"I can do this," she says.

"*We* can do this," I say. "We're in this together. I've got your back."

I feel Elise squeeze my hand a little tighter and she takes a couple of small steps closer to me. I quickly glance down at Maggie and see that she's still in another world with her doll. I look back at Elise, lean my head closer to hers, and see her close her eyes. I can feel my heart racing and the palms of my hands sweating. I close my eyes and lean my head even closer. I've waited for this moment for so very long …

"Just as I suspected!" Dr. Bradshaw says as he walks right past us back in the room. Startled, I quickly pull back from Elise and she does the same. I feel her let go of my hand.

"I had a strong feeling those boys would be gung-ho for another go at it, and I was right. They've already left to take their positions. Are both of you ready?"

"Ready as we're going to be," Elise says.

"All set," I say.

"We're ready, too," Maggie says as she holds Carrie Anne tightly in her arms. "Where do you want us?"

I walk over to Maggie, kneel down in front of her, place my helmet on the ground, and put my arms on her shoulders. "I don't doubt for a second that you and Carrie Anne could take on every single sentry at once and beat them," I say.

Maggie's expression is serious. "We could," she says.

"Oh, I know … but your job on this mission is to stay here and protect this place from any potential invasion that might happen. It's a very important job."

"I accept," Maggie says. "I mean … we accept the mission. We'll keep everything safe from anyone trying to break in."

"I knew I could count on the two of you. You guys make a great team."

Maggie beams with pride. I pick up my helmet, stand, and walk toward the door where Elise is waiting. We walk out together.

"Remember," I hear Dr. Bradshaw say behind me. "Stick to the plan." I pause and look back at him. "And no side adventures," he says.

I nod my head, turn, and walk down the dim corridor with Elise leading the way. Neither of us speak as we walk. My thoughts turn back to Mom and Sarah. I am also overcome with an odd, overwhelming feeling of foreboding, as if some inner voice is trying to tell me something. Perhaps it's trying to tell me that I should just call in sick on this one, to stay home and watch reruns of daytime TV. If only I could. I try to suppress my thoughts and feelings and continue walking.

We reach the back entrance to our safe haven and there is no one to see us off this time. Elise puts her helmet on and I do the same. The helmet quickly powers up, and in what seems like an instant, I can see through the visor. I see Elise touch the controls on her wrist … and then she disappears. The door opens in front of me and a cold blast of air rushes in.

"Are you coming?" I hear Elise's voice ask in my helmet.

"Right behind you."

I walk through the open door, but I'm not entirely sure what I'm walking to. That foreboding feeling washes over me again.

CHAPTER 11

ELISE AND I WALK TO THE OLD bearing factory in near silence, the sounds of our faint footsteps hitting the ground being the only sounds heard. It is bitter cold outside and the freezing air is not only penetrating my suit, it's penetrating my body as well. I don't get far before I start to shiver uncontrollably. I doubt that Elise is faring much better. In our haste to leave as quickly as possible for a second attempt to capture more suits, I completely forgot to wear any extra clothing for warmth.

It's a dreary day, much more so than usual. The thick, dark clouds above look like they are ready to burst with a great deluge at any moment. We see few people on our way and those few who are still out look like they are making their way to shelter. I am starting to have doubts that we are going to even encounter any sentries. They are unlikely to reveal themselves if few or no people are around.

I see the old bearing factory just ahead. It's an eyesore if ever there was one. The brick building is old and has a strong rundown, industrial look to it with its towering smoke stacks, metal staircases that wind up the exterior, and its now-empty receiving docks. I'd say it's well over a hundred years old ... maybe older. It looked old and run down when it was operational when I was young, and it finally closed down before I started high school. It was a common point of reference in years past and we always just called it "the eyesore." The building is in such bad shape these days that I doubt anyone would even consider taking up residence there. Probably the only creatures that call the place home now are the many rats I'm sure infest its dismal interior.

As we approach the derelict old factory, I realize there are very few people in the area around it. This is not what we were expecting and most have probably already left due to the approaching storm. I see a few people trading live chickens, canned food items, and a few other things, but that's about all the activity there is. The dog fights we were expecting don't seem to be happening today. Elise and I take position behind a couple of old cars and wait.

"Doesn't look like there's much activity here today," I say.

"Not yet," Elise says. "But it might pick up. Let's give it a chance."

"Okay, but if there aren't enough people here to harass, the sentries probably won't bother with this area."

"They may or may not. It's hard to say. We should give it some time."

I see Jackson, Riggs, Walker, and Perez attempting to blend in. Riggs and Perez are both talking to vendors, while the other two are sitting on the side of the road, as though they are begging.

"So, what's the story with Jackson, Riggs, Walker, and Perez?" I ask. "Do they have first names or did their mothers not love them?"

Elise giggles. "I'm sure they have first names, but I couldn't tell you what they are. I think going by your last name is some kind of Marine thing, but I'm not sure. They believe in what we're doing, though, I can tell you that much. That's the important thing; that's what really matters."

"If those guys are so tough, why aren't any of them wearing the suits and doing the job we're doing? Doesn't it make more sense for us to be part of the cleanup crew? I mean, why us with all of their military training?"

"We fit the suits and they don't. That's what it comes down to. That will probably change as we acquire more suits, but for now, it's what we have to work with."

I'm not so sure I would say my suit fits all that well. The legs are a little snug, the waist is loose, and the top part feels a little too big. I'm starting to think that each of these suits was custom designed for each individual, although I can't say with certainty. At least that would explain how the incredibly tall sentry I encountered had a suit that actually fit him.

Elise and I continue our vigil, but the activity around the old bearing factory doesn't seem to be picking up. The sky still looks ominous, like it's going to become a terrible storm at any moment, but so far it's holding off. As I sit here waiting for something to happen, I can't help but think about just how close to home I am. It's really not far at all. I could be there in less than ten minutes if I start walking now; maybe even less if I walked quickly. I'm so close, yet so far at the same time. I'm not even sure if I could even call that place my home anymore. I don't see how I can call a place home that I'm forbidden from visiting. I guess the Motor City Community Center is my home now. It does the job well enough, I suppose.

"The community center," I say. "Why was it chosen as a base of operations? Wouldn't a large building like that attract a lot of attention from the sentries?"

"It doesn't, actually. It's just one of many large buildings around the city. The sentries give it a complete pass. You have to understand that they think we're too dumb to organize into anything that would be a threat to them. In their minds, we will always be simple outlanders who aren't smart enough to make it on our own. They think we need them to survive, and they probably just assumed we would be their pawns and punching bags forever."

"Well, they assumed wrong."

I watch as a few more people come and go around the old derelict building. It's as quiet as a mouse here and I really don't think things are going to pick up anytime soon.

"There's not much activity here," I say. "Maybe we should move to the other end of the block. We'll still be close enough to our Marine buddies if and when we need them."

"I agree. There's not much happening here. Maybe we'll have better luck in a new location. It certainly can't hurt to try. Let's go."

Elise and I carefully make our way around the perimeter of the old bearing factory, being careful not to trip on any of the old equipment lying around or to step in any of the mud holes that surround the building. Like most old factories, it's a dangerous place. Accidentally tripping could easily result in being impaled on something or being covered in filth.

It takes us a few minutes, but we make it to our destination, a small area on the other side of the building where people have been known to gather. It is immediately apparent that there isn't any more activity at this location than where we were just a moment ago. In fact, there may be even less. Elise and I take position close to a small group of people trading and wait. A few people come and go. A sickly, stray cat walks by. In the far distance I see the head of a large rat cautiously appear from an old drain pipe. It takes in its surroundings and then quickly disappears into the dark recess it just came from.

I can see my old neighborhood from this side of the building very easily, and I'm now even closer to home than I was just a few minutes ago. Just a few minutes ... that's all I would need to run home, quickly tell Mom and Sarah I'm okay, and then return. Since there is so little activity today, I doubt that it would even matter.

"It's quiet here, too," I say.

"Looks that way. Maybe this wasn't such a good spot after all."

"Elise, we're very close to my home. I'm going to check on my family; I have to. I'll just be a few minutes."

"I don't know if that's such a good idea."

"I have to let them know I'm okay. Besides, there's almost no activity here. I'll be back in no time at all."

"Don't forget what Dad said about side adventures."

"Ten minutes … that's all I need."

"It isn't a good idea, Adam."

"I'll be right back."

I hear a loud sigh of exasperation in my helmet speakers as I walk away from our position and start walking toward my home. This has been a long time coming and I can't wait to see Mom and Sarah's faces, to hug them tightly, and to tell them all that has happened to me.

I just need a few minutes …

CHAPTER 12

I WALK QUICKLY TOWARD MY home and even break out in the occasional slow jog as I go. In my enthusiasm, I completely forget about being cold. I think it's remarkable how being excited about something can completely change how you perceive cold, heat, pain, and so many other things.

My walk home is uneventful and I finally arrive at my destination. Everything looks just as I left it. The paint on the wood siding is chipped and faded, the ceiling is missing shingles, and two broken windows have plastic sheeting over them. It's quite possibly the most beautiful sight I've seen in a long time. I see the flicker of oil lanterns in one of the windows. Smoke rises lazily from the chimney above. It looks so inviting and I can't wait to go in.

I walk up to the front door, grab the doorknob, and pause. I turn and look all around me, not that it would do any good if there are any sentries in the area. I don't see anything that looks unusual. I turn the doorknob, slowly open the door, walk in, and close the door behind me.

Mom is preparing a salad of wild greens. Sarah probably picked them earlier. Sarah is washing clothes in a tub nearby. And Juno ... my dear sweet dog, Juno. I see her sleeping in front of the wood-burning stove. She's lying on her back with her feet in the air and I can hear her snoring.

Mom and Sarah both turn and look in my direction with the sound of the door closing behind me. Mom freezes and a look of fear washes over her. Sarah stops scrubbing the clothes in the tub. Her eyes grow wide and her mouth drops open. And then I realize why I am getting such a reaction. They just witnessed the door open and close on its own. I reach down to my wrist control and disengage stealth.

Mom screams and Sarah jumps up and runs over and stands right next to Mom. They both embrace each other tightly. Juno jumps up from where she was lying and runs over to me. She sniffs my feet and then puts her two front paws up on one of my legs. She lets out a little bark and wags her tail. I reach down and start petting her.

"Hey girl," I say. "I've missed you."

I look up and Mom and Sarah are still holding each other. They still have a look of fear in their eyes, as if they've just seen someone rise from the dead. This isn't the reception I thought I'd get.

And then it suddenly occurs to me that I'm still wearing my helmet. No wonder they aren't acting very enthusiastic about seeing me.

I reach up and practically yank the power cable loose and remove my helmet as quickly as I can.

"It's me, Mom."

Mom gasps loudly.

"Adam?" Sarah asks.

"I'm home," I say.

Mom runs over and wraps her arms around me tightly and I hug her back.

"I'm okay," I say. Mom says something back to me but it just sounds like gibberish since she's now crying heavily. Sarah slowly walks over to me and wraps her arms around me, too. I wrap one of my arms around her and all three of us stand together, holding each other. Juno sits down near my feet and looks up to me with her tongue hanging lazily out of the side of her mouth.

After a moment, we release our embrace. Mom tries to compose herself and she starts wiping tears from her eyes.

"Glad to see you finally decided to grace us with your presence again," Sarah says with a sly grin.

"Couldn't stay away from you," I say.

Sarah laughs. "What happened to your hair?"

"Chopped it off. It's much easier to take care of like this. What do you think about—"

"You can't be here," Mom says in a soft voice.

"I know. I just stopped in for a few minutes to let you know I'm okay."

"There's a manhunt underway for you. They know you live here."

"Mom, I didn't have any choice. I had to kill that sentry. He was about to—"

"Shhh …" Mom says as she puts her hand loosely over my mouth. "I'm sure you had a good reason to do what you did, but that doesn't matter right now." Mom removes her hand from my mouth. "How have you been surviving?" she asks.

"I'm fine. I'm staying with Dr. Bradshaw."

"Richard Bradshaw?"

"Yes."

"You've got to go … now. I'll contact Richard in a few days and check on you. It's not safe for you to be here." Mom looks into my eyes with a look that I've seen countless times growing up. It's a look that says she knows what she's talking about and I had better listen to her. "Go," she says.

She's right, of course. It's definitely not safe here, and I've accomplished all I set out to do by coming here. Mom and Sarah now know I'm okay and they know how to reach me. Mission accomplished. I nod to Mom and then turn around and walk toward the door. I take hold of the doorknob and turn back for another look at my family. I don't know when I'll get to see them again.

"Be careful," Sarah says.

"I will."

With my helmet under one arm, I open the door with my free hand, walk outside, and close it behind me. A blast of cold hits me hard and I can feel the cold air running over my bald head. It's a feeling I'm not used to and I am instantly reminded that I'm not wearing my helmet. I need to hide as quickly as possible. I should have gone into stealth mode before I walked outside. I quickly bring the helmet up to my head and start to put it on.

"Don't move, Adam Reese!" I hear in a loud, deep voice that is coming from somewhere right in front of me. I look all around but see nothing. I don't move. And then ... right in front of me, a sentry appears, an incredibly tall sentry. Is this the same unusually tall sentry I previously encountered? I don't know, but there can't possibly be many others that tall.

The tall sentry slowly walks up to me with his rifle slung across his back and his police baton in hand, ready for action. He comes very close to me, leaving only a few inches between us. I look up into the air at him and he slowly reaches up and removes his helmet, revealing a face I recognize. It is him; it is definitely the sentry I had the encounter with the other day. He looks down into my eyes and grins a wide, mostly toothless grin.

"We meet again, Adam Reese," he says.

I say nothing in response and continue looking up at him.

"And just where did you think you were going?"

Again, I say nothing.

"Well," he says. "You've arrived just in time. The party is about to begin ... and you're the guest of honor. Gentlemen?"

The tall sentry holds both hands up in the air beside him, and then I see another sentry appear nearby. And then another appears on the opposite side. And then another, and another, and another. All around me they appear, one by one ... six of them in all.

I hear Dr. Bradshaw's voice in my head. "No side adventures," he is saying. He was right. I should have listened, but now it may be too late.

CHAPTER 13

"GENTLEMEN," THE TALL SENTRY says with his arms still out by his side. "Standing before us is Mr. Adam Reese. Mr. Reese is accused of a very serious crime, a crime against the king himself."

"Guilty!" one of the sentries exclaims. The other sentries express the same judgment and I hear shouts of "Guilty!" proclaimed all around me.

"Now, let's not be too hasty, gentlemen," the tall sentry says. I do believe a proper trial is in order." The tall sentry lowers his arms and looks down at me again, still smiling.

Thoughts of making a quick escape fill my mind. If I could just find a way to distract them — for just a moment—I could quickly put the helmet on, go into stealth mode, and try to make a break for it. It wouldn't be easy, though. The sentries have me surrounded and it would be difficult to run between them, even if they couldn't see me. The chances of something like that actually working are not very high.

A sentry walks over to me and jerks the helmet I'm carrying out of my hand. "You won't be needing that anymore," he says. So much for my plan.

"Yes," the tall sentry says. "We can be civil about all of this. Check inside the house and bring his family out to witness the trial."

Two sentries go over to the front door and one of them kicks the door hard, forcing it open. The two sentries go inside.

I look around and see a few people watching from a distance. The tall sentry sees them, too. "Come," he says to them. "Come and be witnesses to the trial of Adam Reese." He motions for them to come closer. The people start walking toward us.

Mom and Sarah walk out of our home with the two sentries right behind them. Tears are streaming down Mom's face and she is practically hyperventilating. She knows what's about to happen. Sarah is crying, too. They both stand to the side and hold each other, with one of the sentries right behind them.

I hear a loud, barking sound and see Juno run out of our home. She runs right up to one of the sentries and bites him on the leg while growling loudly. The sentry jerks his leg back hard, but Juno doesn't let go. Her teeth are clenched firmly on her prey. The sentry then raises his baton high above his head, brings it down swiftly, and strikes Juno's body. Juno yelps loudly but doesn't let go. The sentry strikes her again and again. He delivers repeated blows until Juno finally releases the sentry's leg and falls to the ground, writhing in pain, but the sentry doesn't stopping beating my poor pooch. He continues beating her until she stops yelping and there is no more movement. My beloved companion is dead.

I look away from Juno's lifeless body. Seeing her like that is almost more than I can bear. She has been my best friend for so long that I can't even imagine life without her now. On those days when everything looked so bleak and I couldn't see any future for myself, she was right by my side doing everything she could to cheer me up. Some say dogs can sense our emotions, and I believe that to be true. I know it to be true, because Juno did.

I look up at the tall sentry again and see that he is still smiling. He looks over at Juno lying on the ground and laughs. A small crowd of people is now gathering. I recognize some of them from the crowd Elise and I were observing just a few short minutes ago. Jackson, Riggs, Walker, and Perez are among them, too. I see them looking at me with great concern, but there's nothing they can do. As tough as they are, there are just too many sentries for them to handle. I blew it and they know it. The only thing they can do at this point is to stand back and watch the sentries harass me, or worse.

"Adam Reese," the tall sentry says. "You have been accused of killing one of the king's soldiers. How do you plead?"

I say nothing and look straight ahead, into the crowd. I know all of this is for show and it really doesn't matter what I say.

"Very well, then," the tall sentry says. "I will enter a plea of not guilty on your behalf."

The other five sentries break out in laughter around me. Obviously, the idea of me being innocent is something they find very humorous. Mom and Sarah are still embracing each other tightly. Both of their faces are flushed from crying. They know what all of this is leading to.

The tall sentry turns around and faces the other sentries. "Let's consider the evidence, gentlemen," he says. "Mr. Reese was observed committing the act in question by one of our own. When Mr. Reese realized he was being observed, he tried to run to avoid capture. Isn't that correct, Julius?"

One of the sentries steps forward. "That's right; he's the one," he says through his helmet in a deep, distorted voice.

The tall sentry seems pleased with the sentry's answer. He lifts his head in the air and smiles. "The same day our brother was slaughtered was the same day Mr. Reese disappeared. And now he shows up here today wearing one of our infantry suits."

The tall sentry turns back around to me and looks down at me. "Mr. Reese, what do you have to say in your defense?"

Again, I say nothing. I look off to the side and down at the ground. All of this is pointless and they are clearly mocking me with their faux trial.

"The defendant has chosen to remain silent," the tall sentry says as he turns around again to face the other sentries. "Gentlemen, based on the evidence presented to you today, what is your verdict?"

"Guilty!" one of the sentries says. The other sentries join in and refrains of "Guilty!" are heard all around.

The tall sentry turns back to me. "Adam Reese, you have been found guilty of the crime of killing one of the king's soldiers and I hereby sentence you to death."

The tall sentry hits me hard in the stomach with his baton, knocking the breath out of me. I fall to the ground in incredible pain.

"No!" Mom screams loudly. "Take me instead! I beg you!"

"Shut that woman up," the tall sentry says.

Sarah puts her hand over Mom's mouth and tries to hold her back. Mom is clearly hysterical and I wish with everything in me that she and Sarah didn't have to see any of this. It's not up to me, of course. They will force them to watch as part of my punishment, and to instill them with fear.

The tall sentry points his baton at Mom and Sarah. "As for the two of you ... I find both of you guilty of providing aid and comfort to this fugitive. But I'm feeling merciful today. Both of you get to live. You get to live so you can watch Adam Reese die. For the rest of your miserable lives, you get to think about what he has done, and what you have done to help him. From this day forward, you will know real pain, the pain that can only come from suffering.

The tall sentry turns to one of the other sentries and nods to our humble home. "Burn it," he says. He has a look of deep satisfaction, as if he's very pleased with himself.

Mom starts wailing uncontrollably. Sarah is crying loudly, too. Mom falls to the ground and looks up at the tall sentry, begging. "Please, oh, please," she says over and over again. Two people from the growing crowd I don't recognize step forward and pick her up. Each of them put an arm underneath one of Mom's arms and they carry her off, her feet dragging the ground. Sarah follows them, still crying loudly. As they leave the area, Sarah keeps looking back at me, knowing that it will be the last time she will see me alive. The tall sentry watches them leave and laughs. He is enjoying this way too much.

"I need several volunteers to assemble a wooden cross and to help administer the punishment," the tall sentry says to the crowd. "Those who help will be exempt from tributes for a full month."

Several people step forward.

I look at my home and see two sentries walk out of the front door. I see flames leap up the walls on the inside through the door, and then flames burst from the windows. There's no saving it now.

I'm still in incredible pain from the blow I took to my stomach. I hold my belly as I lie on the ground and await my fate. I'm sure it will be a short wait.

CHAPTER 14

THE HOUSE THAT I GREW UP IN—formed so many memories in—is now fully engulfed in flames. It is burning so hot that I can feel the heat from it searing my skin from where I'm lying. The crowd is backing away to get relief from the heat. Juno's lifeless body is lying on the ground nearby. I no longer see Mom and Sarah. They have been taken away from the awful scene unfolding by some very kind people, people I could never thank enough, and will never get the chance to do so. I hear the sound of hammering nearby and I look up and see the volunteers from the crowd—my executioners—hammering away on the wooden cross I'm to be hung from. I have no idea where they got the wood, the hammers, or the nails, nor do I care.

The pain in my abdomen has subsided and I have regained my breath. I try to pick myself up. I bring myself to one knee and try to stand when two sentries come over and hit me hard in my chest, ribs, and head with their batons. Pain shoots through my body and I fall to the ground again. I feel the sensation of water pouring off of my head. Instinctively, I reach up and put my hand in the flowing stream to feel it. It's definitely wet. I lower my hand and take a good look at the fluid dripping from my head. It's crimson red. A steady stream of blood flows off my forehead and runs down my face.

I feel someone or something tugging on my legs and then I feel the same thing happening to one of my arms. I look down at my body and see two of the executioners pulling the sentry suit off me. They are not gentle and they remove the suit forcefully, with no consideration to either me or the suit.

I look all around frantically, but only see outlines of people and buildings. Everything is suddenly blurry, no doubt from the blow I just took to the head. I feel intense anxiety. My heart is beating fast and my breathing is quick and shallow. In a state of confusion, I roll over on my stomach and then bring myself to one knee again. Just as I'm about to try to stand again, I see the outline of a sentry standing over me with his baton raised over his head.

"That's enough!" The tall sentry says. "We don't want to kill him before he receives his real punishment."

The sentry lowers his arm and steps back away from me. I collapse again on the ground.

The sounds of hammering stop. "We're ready," one of the executioners says.

"Proceed with the punishment," the tall sentry says.

Two of the executioners walk over to me, grab my arms, and start dragging me on the ground toward the wooden cross. I let my body go limp in their arms and don't help them in any way.

"Don't make this any harder on yourself than it has to be," one of the men says.

"Easy for you to say," I reply. "As if any of this is easy for me." The man says nothing back to me. He just looks down into my face, expressionless, as though he's just doing a job. My vision is returning and my surroundings are slowly coming into focus.

"You don't have to do this," I say to the two men dragging my body. "Think of what this will do to my family." I don't know why I just said this since it won't do any good. I suppose when times of extreme desperation set in, some will say or do just about anything, regardless of how silly it may be.

"Think of what will happen to our families if we don't do this," one of the men says. "There are no winners in this, Adam. Everyone loses."

The two men continue dragging my body over the rough ground to my destination: the wooden cross. I feel them drag my body onto it. I look up just before the executioners tie me down and see the crowd of people staring at me with a variety of different expressions. Some are looking at me with pity, as though they are genuinely sad to see this happen to me. A few others look shocked and surprised. The majority, however, are expressionless. They've been witnesses to these executions too many times to count and it has become routine to them. I think the fact that far too many people just don't care anymore bothers me more than seeing the sentries laugh at my fate, as though they are genuinely happy to see my demise. I glance over at the tall sentry and see that he is smiling at me. I almost prefer to see someone smile and laugh at me than to be indifferent, to feel nothing at all.

I am now lying on top of the cross on the ground with my arms outstretched. The two men tie one arm down tightly with a strap of leather. They tie it very tight and I can feel it cut into my skin, impeding my circulation. They do the same to my other arm, my legs, and then tie another strap around my waist for good measure. I feel my body being lifted off the ground as they drag the cross over to the hole that was dug just a few moments ago. The men lift me high in the air and then drop the cross into the hole. It jars my body and pain shoots through me. I moan loudly. I hear a loud sound and look up to see the roof of my burning home collapse to the ground below, creating a blast of heat that hits me hard and seems to linger around me. The heat is almost more than I can bear.

"Everyone go home," the tall sentry says. "That's all there is to see."

The crowd of people slowly disperses, but a few people linger behind nearby to watch me struggle and suffer. This is, after all, entertainment to them, something to break the monotony of an otherwise dull existence. I see Jackson, Riggs, Walker, and Perez observing me from a safe distance.

"Julius and Kane," the tall sentry says. "I want both of you to stay here and guard Mr. Reese. We want to make sure no one disturbs him while he thinks about what he has done."

"He has a lot to think about," one of the sentries says. They all laugh.

"Indeed," the tall sentry says. "He does. The rest of you come with me. Our work here is done."

The tall sentry walks off and three of his minions follow. The two remaining sentries take position below me at the base of the cross. I look up again and watch the tall sentry and his minions as they grow smaller in the distance … and then they disappear in stealth mode, one by one.

I am now alone and have only my thoughts to keep me company. Maybe the sentries were right when they said I have a lot to think about. I am overcome with a strong feeling of regret and guilt for the choices I made that led to this. Because of my poor decisions, Mom and Sarah no longer have a home and my passing will cause them a great deal of suffering. My beloved dog, Juno, is now dead; the sentries have one of their suits back in their possession, and our mission to retrieve two more sentry suits is now a total failure. And it's all my fault. I have caused a great deal of anguish to my friends and family and have absolutely no one but myself to blame. It is a burden that weighs heavily on me as I hang on this cross in intense pain, struggling to breathe. Maybe I deserve this ... or maybe I don't. I don't know. At this point I can't change anything; I can't do anything to make amends.

All of this is my fault and it is my cross to bear.

The Detroitopia saga continues!

Be sure to check out the next installment, My Cross To Bear, to see what happens next!